Copyright © 2018 by JB Michaels

All rights reserved.

No part of this book may be reproduced in any form or by any
electronic or mechanical means, including information storage and
retrieval systems, without written permission from the author, except
for the use of brief quotations in a book review.

❀ Created with Vellum

Jane Fae Flyer is tasked with an impossible mission: Find three missing fairies in the most surveilled and secure city in the world, Washington D.C.

From the mind of USA Today bestselling author, JB Michaels, comes his most harrowing thriller yet, A Capitol Abduction.

Taking place just days after the Spiritless invasion of the North Pole was thwarted by the Tannenbaum Tailors and Fairy Fleet combined, a new crisis emerges.

Jane will need to reunite with her estranged sister to accomplish her objective. Will the sisters put aside their differences for the greater good?

Suspense, danger, and intrigue abound in a fantasy action thriller that will take you on dizzying flight from the Washington Monument to the Smithsonian to the Statue of Freedom.

Fly Fast. Fly Strong in A Capitol Abduction.

For Irene, the most caring and courageous ever.

For all the women in my life, whose power and persever-ance inspire me.

CONTENTS

ONE

INTERRUPTED SLEEP

Jane's wings ached. She flapped her wings repeatedly hoping to work out the sting. The damage from the South Pole's wind pervaded her every thought, emotion, movement. The events of the past Christmas might have changed her forever. A fairy's wings are a fairy's identity. She hoped that with wing therapy and exercises the pain would lessen over time.

She didn't have time for pain.

The Fae Flyer's pride lay in her ability to lead, to command, to fly among her fellow Fae with a sense of confidence that pushed her to being one promotion away from Admiral.

She stood in front of her bathroom mirror. Jane removed her leather aviator helmet and pushed her fingers through her hair and rubbed her scalp. Her blond hair was a knotted, curly mess. She sighed blowing her hair from her face with an overlapped bottom lip and jutted chin. She examined her dirty, rosy-blemished face. Jane sighed again.

Exhaustion weighed on her like a ton of bricks. Missions like the one she just flew having thwarted another Spiritless assault had sapped her strength.

It was time to rest.

Jane couldn't find the energy to shower. She took off her jacket and sat down on the sink to remove her boots. She kicked off the right and struggled with the left one. Her hammock looked like heaven. Jane slipped off the sink and fell on her butt.

"Ugh. Just what I needed. Nice work, Jane. Nice. Work."

She sat on the floor and pushed the boot off then dragged herself over to the hammock, folded her wings and lay down. Within seconds she was out.

The vibration of her phone rattled on her desk. The phone's silent but physically obnoxious function caused it to fall off her desk and onto the floor, where it still shook.

Jane's eyes cracked open.

"Ugh! I just fell asleep!" The fairy grabbed for her phone still in her hammock. She swung herself to the phone and picked it up.

"Hello..."

"Jane. I need you come down to the hangar," a male voice burst from the speaker.

"I was just there...what could have possibly happened? I just fell asleep." Jane rubbed her forehead.

"Jane it's been about 14 hours since you left here. I need you back here now, that's an order."

"Yes, sir. Right away." Jane ended the call. Admiral Pixie's tone was far too serious and panicked. He was her commanding officer, but he usually acted so casual and aloof that it frustrated her. Something must have rattled him. Jane rolled herself out her hammock and stretched her wings, then went back to rubbing her head. Her headache was bad, not a full migraine but close enough. Her bottle of DUST was depleted. She took too much of it anyway. She will have to deal with the bad headache and the fatigue of perhaps, sleeping too long.

Jane walked over to the mirror and quickly put her hair up in a ponytail. She splashed her face with some cold water, secured her helmet and boots and was off.

TWO
FAILURE TO REPORT

Jane's wings still stung from her last adventure. She flew a little slower to lessen the pain and enjoy the journey. The Fairies' Hollow was just outside the North Pole's residential trees where the tree elves lived. She flew through a tunnel of ice and tree bark that were lit up by tracking lights all the way to the outside. The round bulbs were colored blue and yellow and they gently flashed, as to provide a sense of peace for the Fae who lived in North Pole Hollow. Jane reached the tunnel's end. The view still took her breath away, even after flying out of it her whole life. The North Pole's residential pine trees blinked and beamed with the colors of the rainbow.

The tree elves really know how to decorate their ornamental homes, each tree with a different combination of two colors. Jane passed the Western tree's orange and red lights and ahead was the North Tree's blue and gold bulbs. The smaller residential trees surrounded the massive, majestic, Home Tree: the official Tannenbaum Tailor headquarters for tree elves that maintain Christmas trees in human homes every year.

Beyond the grand circle of Christmas trees is North Pole City. The supreme craftsmanship and immersive detail made the North Pole's buildings incredible. The Workshop's multi-colored and ever-changing spectrum of colors was a sight to see and representative of the work always being done inside its hallowed halls: toy research and development, new decorative technologies, all refined and innovated to raise and maintain Christmas spirit levels.

Everything had a purpose. Every building's architecture conveyed a message. The only exception was the hangar to the outside of the city center, where the fairies worked alongside Tannenbaum Tailor pilots and their Icicle ships. It was just a massive half-cylinder and was purely functional. Jane sighed. She could have used a few days away from work.

She flew into the hangar bay. The maintenance teams were flying around, touching up the Tannenbaum Tailors' Icicle ships. All around Jane hover engines fired. The noise was loud, and it did not help Jane's headache. Her head pounded. She winced and pulled her leather helmet down farther. Its cushion was no match for the decibels of noise.

Pixie's office was elevated over the rest of the hangar bay. Jane landed on the catwalk and could see him sitting and looking out the window. He must have sensed her presence and stood to greet her.

"Someone's eager to see me." Jane landed on the catwalk next to Pixie's office.

Pixie opened his door, "Come in and have a seat."

Jane sunk into the cushy comfortable office chair.

"Okay what's going on? Anyone else going to join us or no?"

"Right now, I think its best we keep this to ourselves and then we can decide who else we want to include. Most of the Tailor Icicles have returned or are accounted for. All the Flyers have reported in as well, with the exception of three Fairies. Three Tailor teams have reported their flyer's disappearance."

Jane took her helmet off and leaned forward in the chair. Pixie paced behind his desk.

"So, three fairies have disappeared?! Are they connected in some way? Where were their mission areas?" Jane asked.

"Yes, they were all on duty in the Washington, D.C. metro area. Now they are gone. I brought you in because you are my best flyer. D.C. is the most surveilled city in America. I can't send the entire fleet to search but we can't have fairies flying all over the nation's capital. I need you to find them and bring them home." Pixie put his hands on his desk and gave a worried look to Jane. She could see the tired lines around his eyes. He hadn't slept. She felt guilty about the 14 hours of sleep she just enjoyed.

Jane straightened up in her chair.

"Yes, sir."

THREE
DETAIL AND DETAIL

"With the attempted Spiritless invasion of the NP, the Home Tree's communications were shut down, the Tailor teams attempted to report the missing Fae after they exhausted their search for them in their respective assigned trees and human homes." Pixie examined the report in the middle of his desk, glasses balanced on the end of his nose.

"They came back to make the reports and their trees were probably taken down. It's their protocol. I understand that." Jane leaned over to look at the report as well.

"The Tailor teams who reported were devastated and worried. They are overwhelmed with news of the thwarted Spiritless invasion. Still you should pay them all a visit," Pixie said.

"The timeline is interesting. A fairy goes missing

on December 23rd, then two in rapid succession on the 25th," Jane said.

"That is really all we know at this point. I would suggest recruiting another flyer to accompany you on the investigation."

"I have someone in mind already. I just hope she isn't as sore as I am."

"I will have the Tailor teams here for further questioning when you get back." Pixie said.

"COCO, YOU HOME?" Jane knocked on Coco's round door in North Pole Hollow.

No answer.

Jane knocked again, a little harder this time. Jane noticed a light turn on in through the small window in the door.

"Hold on...ouch...ugh." Coco's dark brown hair covered most of her face. She attempted to brush it back as she opened her door slowly.

"Are you as exhausted as I am?" Jane asked, happy to see her fellow Fae Flyer.

"I think I may be more... I just used the power Frenetic to and from the Spiritless' South Pole lair in the last week." Coco chuckled.

Jane felt the instinct to act as Coco's superior officer but, instead hugged her dear friend.

9

"Thank you so much for braving the journey. Without you, the North Pole would be lost." Jane's eyes teared up as she held Coco close.

"It was my duty. I was just doing my job. Ouch."

"Oh gosh! Sorry I know you are sore!" Jane finally let go.

"I am so sorry to bother you, but we have a problem and if you are physically able, I could use your help, actually, three fairies and their families could use your help."

Coco looked at her bandaged burned wing. A firework display from a human theme park had injured the wing on her journey back to the North Pole.

"I should be good to go."

FOUR
THE DISAPPEARANCES

The two fairies flew back to the Hangar and to Pixie's office where the Tailor teams who reported the missing fairies awaited them.

"How was that flight? You okay?" Jane asked Coco.

Jane could tell Coco tried to show no signs of physical pain. Her friend winced as she landed on the catwalk to Pixie's wood-paneled office raised high above the Icicle ships below.

"I take that as a no," Jane said.

"No, I will be all right. Just a little sore is all." Coco slowly flapped her wings.

"I think we will have to take a training shuttle for this mission. Besides it would be better anyway considering we don't know what shape our missing are in." Jane walked into Pixie's office and saw the tree elves sitting in a semi-circle around Pixie's desk.

"Welcome back Jane. Esteemed tree elves this is Jane, the best flyer in the fleet, she will be heading up the investigation."

The Tannenbaum Tailors, or tree elves, in the room nodded and said hello, some waved, others vocalized, there was a pervasive sense of despair in their demeanor. The expression on their faces were sullen and their shoulders slumped.

"Hello, meet Coco, my assistant. She will be aiding me in the investigation."

Again, the same unenthusiastic greeting.

"We feel terrible. We're so sorry," a Tailor said.

"There is no need to be sorry. We just could use some more specific details on the first disappearance. Who was there when that happened on the 23rd?" Jane asked.

"It was my team. I am Captain Cory. We were doing routine checks. Our fairy, Veronica, was calling out areas of our tree that needed attention..."

Jane interrupted, "Where exactly was Veronica? Was she hovering around the tree? On the interior of the tree?"

"She was hovering outside of the tree. The humans had gone to sleep, and we felt the need to do some extra work. Veronica liked to help and with her fairy's-eye view we could really identify areas of need on the tree, whether it be an ornament, or drooping branch, etc.," Cory said.

"She was hovering outside of the tree when she disappeared?" Jane prodded.

"We were talking when suddenly her com went out. That was it. It just crackled to a stop. She was gone. My ornament Tailor found this on the end of one of the branches." Captain Cory held up Veronica's communicator, a small earpiece.

"So, you or your crew didn't see anything at all. She was just gone in a flash and all that was left was her communicator?" Jane asked.

"That is correct. We scoured every inch of our tree." Captain Cory lowered his head.

"Where was your tree assigned?"

"The residence of the United States' President."

"The White House?" Jane's eyes went wide.

"Yes, that's correct."

FIVE
RAPID SUCCESSION

Captain Cory put his head in his hands.

Jane reeled from the recent reveal. The White House, one of humanity's most guarded compounds on Earth, if not the most secure, was the scene of an abduction. This complicated the investigation immensely.

"What about the other two missing Fae?" Jane looked for the other Captains.

A female tree elf spoke, "Captain Julia here. We lost our fairy in a similar fashion. We were stationed at a tree in the National Press Club's lobby on December 25th at roughly the same time, 0600, as the second fairy that went missing on that day."

Another Tailor Captain spoke up, "Captain Will here, yes my team was stationed at the Smithsonian Museum of American History. Same way as the other two, fairy was in flight at the time of her disappearance."

"Did you two find their communicators like Cory did?"

"No, we did not." The Tailor Captains answered.

"So you both recorded their disappearances at roughly the same time?"

"Yes, within a few minutes of each other in the 0600 hour."

"All the disappearances occurred at times when there would be little or no human interference. The manner of their abductions while in mid-flight or hovering patterns: You all saw nothing in regard to their disappearance? They were just gone?"

"Yes, we wish we could say we did see something. However, there is a chance that the surveillance cameras at each location will be able to tell us more." Captain Julia leaned forward in her chair.

"If it was a human you surely would have all seen the person. It had to have been another type of Fae," Jane said.

"Perhaps but let's not jump to any conclusions. Tailor Captains thank you for your time," Admiral Pixie stood up from behind his desk. The Tailor Captains stood to leave the room, Captain Cory stopped and said to Jane and Coco, "If we can be of any assistance during the investigation just let us know."

"What do you need from me?" Admiral Pixie shut the door.

"There is no way that Coco and I are going to be able to fly down to D.C. in our state. We have just been through hell fighting the Spiritless. We will need a shuttle for sure," Jane said.

"Yes, that would be nice." Coco sat down.

Admiral Pixie observed the two willing fairies, Jane noticed the look on his face questioned whether they were able, "You sure you don't want me to get a couple other fairies on this?"

Coco's bandaged wing looked like it hurt a lot. Jane's eyes could not hide her exhaustion.

"No, no. Just give us the shuttle and we will be on our way."

SIX

SHUTTLING

In the corner of the Icicle Hangar were the emergency shuttles, used for Fairy Frenetic training. Using Fairy Frenetic Power was very dangerous. It causes the Fairy to fly at incredible speeds by utilizing an ancient method of acceleration and aerodynamics. Jane and Coco had mastered it. Using it for extended periods of time can cause injury and dangerous fatigue.

The shuttles were used to collect the fairies who failed at mastering the power Frenetic. However, the shuttles were used at the North Pole Hollow training facilities and had not ever been used for long-distance travel.

"Are you sure you want to use one of these things?" Admiral Pixie pulled on the doorway hatch of the rectangular, hover shuttle. He walked towards the angled cockpit and switched on the power. A series of beeps echoed throughout the empty shuttle. The shuttle then started to vibrate. Jane and Coco looked at each other.

"Oh, don't worry the vibrating will stop in about a minute. It has to go through its power cycling first. You should have enough fuel to make it down there and back. There are reserves in the corner if you need them." Admiral Pixie pointed to the sterile white cargo area of the shuttle.

"Thanks Admiral. We can take it from here," Jane said.

"Okay keep me updated. Anything you need. Just let me know." Admiral Pixie closed the shuttle door.

Jane and Coco looked at each other.

"What the heck are we doing?" Coco laughed.

"We are taking a rickety old shuttle to Washington, D.C., to save our fellow fairies and I have no idea if we will make it." Jane laughed and took her aviator helmet off.

Coco grabbed the flight wheel and engaged the hover thrusters. They floated in the corner and observed the thousands of Icicles in the hangar.

"Why can't we just use an Icicle?" Coco asked.

"Only Tailors know how to fly those things. Pixie wants us to keep this internal. After the Spiritless invasion, he did not want to cause more panic in the Pole.

We would have been able to fly down if we were healthy enough. The shuttle will be fine," Jane said.

Coco moved the shuttle to the open the hangar doors.

"But some Tailors already are involved?"

"You are right, we just have to follow orders, I suppose, if Pixie wanted us to take an Icicle he would have offered."

The shuttle shook some more as Coco fired the forward thrusters.

"Yikes. Well, here we go."

"No, we have to make one stop before we go. We need to see Lily, my favorite Pilot and Communications Tailor first."

"Aren't we supposed to keep this between everyone in that meeting? And, again, another Tailor involved. This is not making much sense, Jane," Coco said.

"I know, I know, but Lily is an exception. She can give us a unique advantage. Lily is key."

SEVEN
LILY ENHANCED

Coco flew the shuttle out of the Hangar and into the cold air of the North Pole. Jane saw the North Pole's buildings and treetops were below. Blinking lights in brilliant, flowing patterns like some of humanity's Christmas displays except, these lights were not an imitation but the real deal. The hangar grew smaller and smaller as they ascended.

"Okay let's head to the Home Tree. I will hail Lily with the shuttle's com." Jane pressed a microphone button and punched in Lily's elfphone number. The speaker on the shuttle was tinny, but good enough as the phone rang.

"Lily here. Over."

"Lily! You answer your phone like you are on the job! Really?!" Jane laughed.

"Oh, hey Jane! Yes, sorry it's just a habit. I can't

seem to get out of work mode after a mission, especially this year. What can I do for you?"

"I have to bring you on a top-secret mission Coco and I have been assigned to. Can we meet at the base of the Home Tree in about five minutes?"

"What do you mean?" Lily asked.

"I would like it very much if we discussed this in person. I am sure you have much to do. I just need you to hear me out. I owe you one. You know I wouldn't ask for help unless I really needed it," Jane said.

"Yes, frankly, I am surprised you are asking for my help. Absolutely, let me grab my GlimmerLift and I will be right down there." Lily ended the call.

Coco pointed to the Home Tree. "Do you want me to land? Or keep us hovering at the base of the tree?'"

"Keep us hovering. We should bring her aboard for a few minutes then drop her back off."

Coco descended. The massive, centrally-located, Fraser fir Home Tree loomed larger the closer they flew to it. The lights and ornaments sparkled and shined; round, sparkling reds, blues, yellows, and greens. The Garland Express hummed with tree-elf traffic. There was movement everywhere in the tree. It was a like observing an entire downtown area of a major city, just in a Christmas tree.

"Okay I will keep us here." Coco maintained a

stable hover just below the lowest branch of the Home Tree.

"There she is." Jane pointed to Lily who was rappelling to the ground with her grappling hook that tree elves use to traverse pine trees, the GlimmerLift.

"I will go pick her up." Jane opened the shuttle door and flew out.

"Here we are," Jane flew in with Lily.

"Okay, what do you need from me? Really like your scarf by the way."

"Thanks, Brendan got it for me for Christmas. He gives really great gifts."

"He does. Okay sorry. What's happening?" Lily asked.

"We may need your help getting schematics and info for three buildings in D.C. The National Press Club, Smithsonian Museum of American History, and well, The White House. Also, this shuttle, any tips or suggestions on how to best use this thing?"

"I can get you info on those buildings with my GlimmerHack. D.C. has an interconnected system of computers and I can see what files they have stored there. Maybe I can find some schematics. I mean this is some serious work you are asking me to do. Borderline problematic and against protocols, you know?"

"Yes, I understand the risks but it's worth the risk.

You mean they have the internet now?" Jane attempted to brush off Lily's point.

Lily paused for a moment then let her worries go. "It appears humans are finally starting figure out the internet. I mean it is nearly 1989. As far as this shuttle, don't expect to get to D.C. very fast. You will burn through the battery charge really fast. Take it easy and I would bring an extra charger, just in case."

She checked the charge gauge on the dash to the right of Coco.

"Okay so you have our com numbers. Anything else we need?" Jane asked.

Lily fished through her pants pockets and found five small candy canes. "These shouldn't be too conspicuous...haha. These are amplified relays. Put these on any antennae or satellites on the buildings you explore, and I should be able to hack in and hold the connection easily."

"Okay, just lick and stick?" Jane laughed.

"These candy canes are not to be consumed. Just hook them on to any part of antennae on the building. Ya know, a conductor."

"Well, thank you Lily. We shall be in touch."

Coco landed the shuttle right where Lily rappelled.

"I look forward to it. I suppose I am on a need to know protocol?" Lily asked.

"We will be in touch Lily. Thank you." Jane patted the tree elf's back.

Lily stepped off the shuttle and gave a thumbs up, "Remember you will have to go at a steady speed or you will drain the battery!"

Coco and Jane gave a reciprocal thumbs up as they left the Home Tree proper.

EIGHT
TURBULENCE

"So, this thing runs on batteries. That's comforting!" Coco's eyes were wide as she guided the shuttle out of North Pole Airspace.

Jane raised from the co-pilot seat and checked the cargo area. There was a large rectangular box with a blinking yellow light and another next to it with a green light.

"We seem to have two batteries. One we are currently using and one we can use for backup. They are big batteries and I think we should be okay if we maintain a steady speed. I would just put it on auto-pilot. It will take us a while to get there. Maybe we can even get some rest." Jane sat back down in the co-pilot seat.

The vast glaciers of the North Pole were below

them. A group of polar bear cubs tackled and played with each other below.

Coco flipped the auto-pilot switch on. "This is gonna take a while but at least we don't have to fly ourselves. I just don't think I could do it."

"Me neither. This is crazy. I have never been so sore. We went through some pretty intensive training in Flight school." Jane leaned back in her chair and stretched her wings and rubbed her left shoulder. Jane felt the need to engage in small talk. She had been serious and always stressing the importance of the mission with Coco since they first met. Being her superior officer means it would be up to Jane to engage the conversation.

"So why did you join the fleet, Coco?"

"I wanted to serve. My parents served. And well..." Coco hesitated.

Jane didn't know if she should prod any further. "Well, my Dad served too and that is why I joined. He really didn't push me into it though. He wanted me to come into it on my own. So, I did it and I love it."

"I am sorry, I guess I never told anyone this story before, come to think of it, but my older sister was helping me learn how to fly when I was a kid. She was the best and was obsessed with the Fleet. I had difficulty with directional control at first and flew too close to the Home Tree Highway. My sister saved me from getting hit by a gift boxcar but, in the process got hit and died." Coco's brown eyes teared up.

Jane froze. A few seconds passed. Jane finally said, "I am sorry."

"You don't have to be sorry. It has led me to this amazing career of helping and serving the North Pole. I just wanted to do something to help prevent situations like that. My goal is to be the head instructor at Flight School someday." Coco smiled wiping a tear from her cheek.

"Well that is an admirable way to honor your sister's sacrifice. I am sure she would be proud. You are lucky to have had such a great sister. Why don't you lay down in the back I will monitor the airways?"

"I think I will take you up on that."

"Oh, it's an order." Jane smiled.

Jane's newfound understanding of what motivated Coco made her feel an even stronger connection with her friend. Their friendship had been forged by the fires of a secret mission to the South Pole to infiltrate the Spiritless lair. Jane was then captured by the dark elves and Coco flew pole-to-pole to save her and Christmas. The least Jane could do is give her some time to rest.

JANE'S CHIN dipped to her chest.

She shook the sleep from her body or she thought she did, the shuttle vibrated. Jane quickly grabbed the flight stick to wrest control and try to avoid any further turbulence. Her head throbbed from the violent dips up and down. The shuttle's walls rattled. The internal cargo compartment doors shook open.

"Whoa, that is some intense turbulence." Coco helped Jane with the flight stick.

"Can we get under or over it?" Jane asked.

"I don't think there is much we can do, but just keep the shuttle in the air. I got this." Coco secured her seatbelt in the pilot's chair and took the controls from Jane.

Another violent drop. Jane's stomach felt like it was in her throat and then forced its way down to her knees.

"Is it me or does this not seem like normal turbulence?!" Jane yelled.

Coco tried to turn the plane. The stick moved but the view in the view port stayed the same, marking no change in direction. They were above a raging river which emptied into what looked like a massive waterfall.

"We keep dipping up and down. I might fricking puke," Jane said. She checked the compass on the flight console. "Aren't we supposed to be heading South, Coco?!"

"Yes, of course. I know it says North. I don't have control of the shuttle at all."

The scream rattled the fairies' ear drums.

"What the heck was that?" Jane put her hands over the flaps of her aviator helmet that covered her ears.

The shuttle dropped again. They were still above the river, headed to the falls.

Coco and Jane could not believe their eyes. An eagle's talon smashed through the viewport and jutted into the ceiling of the shuttle. The talon was dark grey, large, and sharp enough to end a fairy's life in one stab.

Coco fell out of her pilot's seat narrowly dodging the massive bird-of-prey's natural weaponry.

They had lost control of the shuttle to a screaming eagle.

NINE
EAGLE FLIGHT

"EEEEEEEEEEEEEEEEEEEE!"

Another scream assaulted their ears. An eagle had captured them in mid-air and had taken them off-course, off-mission. To Jane this was unacceptable.

Jane and Coco huddled near the back of the shuttle.

"Well, this is my fault. I fell asleep. Darn eagle. Where do you think we are?" Jane asked.

The cold wind whipped around the cabin of the shuttle entering through the broken viewport.

"We are heading north you said. And we are above a raging river that is heading towards falls, right?" Coco said.

"Coco spit it out!" Jane commanded.

"I am trying to think. I think we must be heading

towards Niagara Falls. It makes sense since Niagara, in general, is between the NP and D.C. but why is the eagle leading us right to falls. What the heck does the eagle want with us anyway?!"

"Maybe it thinks we're a flying fish. We need to punch the heck out this talon." Jane stood up and grabbed a hold of the talon that was piercing the ceiling from the broken viewport. It did nothing but cause the eagle to plunge its other talons deeper into the sides of the shuttle. Both sides of the shuttle jutted inward.

"Great. We have to fly out of here. But now the door's busted." Jane let go of the talon.

"We can try getting out the front viewport. There isn't much room but it's our only shot!" Coco stood up and started to flap her wings.

The eagle shook the shuttle once more. Coco and Jane bounced up and down, then rolled side to side.

"Unbelievable!" Jane yelled. Coco screamed as her burnt wing took even more damage.

The eagle's talon retreated from the cabin.

"Now is the time to make our move out of here!" Jane tried to help Coco to her feet. Coco had gripped the side of the rectangular battery in pain from the turbulent ride.

Jane's eyes grew wider as she realized what happened. The shuttle was in free fall.

"Hang on Coco!" Jane covered Coco and gripped the battery as well.

Jane felt the sensation of falling mixed with nausea. She gasped then held her breath. The shuttle spun as it descended then bobbed right before smacking into the cold Niagara River.

TEN
SUBMERSIBLE

Jane and Coco lost their grip on the battery and hit the ceiling of the shuttle before slamming back to the floor of the shuttle.

"I hope this thing can float. You okay, Coco?" Jane's hope diminished quickly as water began to pour in through the viewport. The frigid Niagara river sprayed into the shuttle and quickly covered the floor.

"I could be way better. I will be honest." Coco stood up just as the water was about to hit her face and torso.

"Okay we need to get out of here before we hit the falls. I don't think we will survive that fall. That is a foregone conclusion."

"Do we let this fill up and then swim out when it's full?" Coco asked. The force of the water that penetrated the shuttle was too strong to take head-on.

"We don't have a choice. Right now, we are still on the surface but won't be for long."

The shuttled bobbed up and down in the rapids of the Niagara river. The sun intermittently illuminated the cabin. The water hadn't weighed down the shuttle enough to sink just yet.

"We still may have some power in this old thing. If we punch it, we may be able to get us out of the water long enough to fly out on our own power." Coco splashed through to the console. The shuttle bobbed again. Water poured in and hit Coco hard. She held on to the flight stick. The water receded as they bobbed up due to the rapids.

"I hope the controls haven't been completely destroyed. Jane hang on!"

Jane grabbed the battery again. Coco pushed the flight stick forward.

Jane winced then shut her eyes expecting a surge. Nothing happened. Just more bobbing.

"Well that didn't work! We need to get out of here now!" Jane flapped her wings.

Coco did the same. Jane flew to the viewport and the shuttle tipped forward. She hit the ceiling hard, again. The shuttle stopped its continuous undulation and now tipped into the abyss. The water poured in.

Coco trudged through waist deep water and joined Jane near the viewport.

The temperature of the water caused Coco's teeth to chatter. The Niagara in December was unfit for swimming. When flying, fairies do run considerably warmer than humans. Coco and Jane needed to fly.

"Take a deep breath." Jane recovered from yet another slam in the interior of the shuttle and looked into Coco's eyes. "We can do this."

The water was now at Coco and Jane's shoulders. They began to tread water. The shuttle still moved forward through the water even though it was sinking fast. The Niagara river doesn't stop for anyone or anything. The magnificent and malevolent falls lay ahead.

ELEVEN
SINK OR FLY

Jane went under first. Coco followed. The shock of the water's temperature diminished as survival mode kicked in. Jane pushed through the view port. She used her wings to propel through the water. The raging current made her go even faster towards the falls. She turned to see if Coco had made it out. There was no way to see Coco. Jane had to pull herself out of the water or she wouldn't make it. The current was too strong to fight against. She had to ride it up and out of the water.

Jane emerged from the water in dramatic fashion. Her wings glowed with the Power Frenetic. The sunlight provided only minimal comfort as the cold air felt like it bore down to her marrow. She was going to freeze to death if she didn't keep moving.

She looked for Coco. Jane noticed that she

emerged about twenty feet from the falls. Still no Coco.

She considered diving back in. Her heart sank as she looked around frantically.

She secured her aviator goggles to her eyes. Took a deep, brisk, breath and began her dive.

"EEEEEEEEEEEEEEEEEEEE!"

Jane slowed up.

"You have got to be kidding me?" Jane stopped and hovered an inch from hitting the water. She knew that eagles were masters at fishing prey from bodies of water.

The eagle dove for her.

"What is your deal?" Jane swerved up and away from the plummeting bird-of-prey.

The eagle spread its wings to slow its descent and followed Jane.

"EEEEEEEEEEEEEEEEEEEEEE!"

Jane considered flying back over the river but chose the opposite direction. She dove over the falls towards the spray of the massive whitewater falls.

"Come and get me down here!" Jane ignored her seemingly frozen state and sore wings.

The eagle didn't hesitate. It turned around and dove in the same direction of the falls with only a few feet between it and the falls themselves.

Jane turned and couldn't see through the spray of

the falls. Jane hovered in cover where the falls ended. If she couldn't see the eagle, the eagle couldn't see her.

Her wings steadily flapped. The spray pelted her entire body. She didn't know much longer she could stay in the polar spray.

Jane felt immense pressure around her torso then ascended swiftly. It took her a few seconds to realize what happened. She was caught in the eagle's talon. She was high above the falls and far away from her friend.

TWELVE
PREDATOR

Jane could barely move. Her arms and wings were pinned in the eagle's grip. The eagle flew her back over the Niagara river. She was looking down. She hoped that Coco was alive and could possibly see her signal.

Jane clicked her boots together. The fairy DUST smokescreen sprinkled out over the mighty river, leaving a trail for Coco to follow. Even in the sun the sparkling cloud of DUST was visible.

"Oh, please Coco. Please. Be alive."

She clicked her heels together again. More DUST puffed from her boots. The eagle had no discernible destination. Jane only saw the river beneath her. The river's contours seemed to move in her view. The eagle had changed direction and now headed over land. Snow-covered trees peppered the landscape below Jane and her captor.

"EEEEEEEEEEE!" The eagle sped up as if close to home and tightened its grip on Jane.

Pain ran like a hot streak through Jane's frigid body. The tightened grip diminished Jane's hope for escape and Coco. She could barely breathe. She clicked her boot heels again then closed her eyes.

"Jane! Jane!" The fairy flyer opened her eyes to a friendly call. Jane smelled straw and sticks and looked down. She was half-buried. Her torso was free, next to a giant eagle egg. She was in the eagle's nest.

"Jane. We gotta get you outta here. Help me get you loose!" Coco pulled at the tangled straw of the nest.

"You are alive! How in the heck did you get out of there?" Jane asked delighted to see her fellow Fae.

"I was actually right behind you when the eagle dove for you. I flew higher than you when we initially left the shuttle. To steer clear of the falls. The eagle literally pounded your body into this nest. Are you able to move at all?" Coco struggled.

The eagle's scream rattled their fairy ears. It was returning to the nest.

"I am not leaving." Coco dropped the straw she had pulled to loosen Jane's bonds and flew out and under the nest.

"Yes, hide. That is good. I can handle this big dumbass eagle. All tied up. I got this." Jane sighed.

The eagle landed on a branch next to the nest. It's left eye scoured the nest. It cocked its head as it could tell Coco had tampered with Jane's straw prison.

"What do you want with me?" Jane yelled to the eagle.

The eagle moved its beak closer to Jane.

"All this for lunch. I mean you could have eaten me a long time ago!"

Another eagle screamed on approach.

"Oh, I am not for you. I am for your companion. Great. Just great."

The second eagle was smaller and looked into Jane's eyes then screamed.

"What is with all the screaming? I have a headache!" Jane didn't stop fighting. Ever.

The smaller eagle bent down further to examine Jane before it's beak would assuredly pierce and kill Jane.

"Just do it...." Jane felt like she was sinking into quicksand. Coco pulled her through the bottom the nest.

"Wow! That was amazing!" Jane said.

"Will you shush. We don't want to end up back in the nest." Coco put a finger over her lips.

"Right. Right. Sorry." Jane hovered next to Coco underneath the branch.

Jane, "What do we do..." Coco shook her head.

The eagles screamed again then ascended from the branch.

Coco peeked out from underneath the nest. Then signaled the 'all clear.'

"Thank you so much! I owe you again."

Jane flew toward Coco intent on giving her a big hug. She noticed a blur in the left side of her field of vision. Then Coco vanished as the blur overtook her friend.

THIRTEEN
REVOLVING

This day could not have been any worse. Attacked and abducted by eagles and now Coco vanished before her eyes.

The blur must have been another fairy using the power Frenetic. Jane flew in the general direction she thought the abductor had gone, but it was no use. The blur and Coco were gone.

The frigid air engulfed Jane who was still wet from the polar plunge into the mighty Niagara. She had no deicing lamps for her wings. She remembered she had taken them off and threw them onto the floor of her house back at the North Pole Hollow. She had been so exhausted.

Jane had to find some shelter and somehow dry her clothes.

Jane grabbed for the communicator inserted in her

ear. She tapped on it hoping to hear a pinging sound that would denote its functional state. Nothing. It may have not survived the shuttle's dive.

Jane's eyes moistened with tears. She realized she had lost track of where she was. She hovered near the forest floor and rubbed her head. Jane quickly flew above the tree-line to get her bearings then back down.

"Jane. You got this." She flew towards the river. She maintained low altitude as to avoid another eagle attack. Flight made the cold air's effect worse. Much worse. She neared the river and turned toward the falls. She flew as fast as she could without using the Power Frenetic. Her fatigue and general soreness still lingered and hampered her. If she could get some more rest, her fairy body could heal itself rather efficiently. There was just no time. One crisis to the next, Jane's grit would have to endure greater stress.

She could see the resort area that boasted views of the falls to those with deep enough pockets to pay for a view of nature's grandeur.

"Hotel Niagara. That's creative." Jane read the sign nestled along the side of the deluxe resort she flew toward. Hotel Niagara was a curved tower. A half circle with the outside of the circle facing the falls.

Jane flew to the front entrance. The grand awning proved a spectacle itself with a brilliant 'Hotel Niagara' sign lit with big clear bulbs as if on old Broadway. Jane flew to the revolving door, hovered near the ceiling waiting for an opening. She purposely picked a section of the revolving door that was empty until at the very last second a human child hopped into the doorway much to her parent's chagrin. They yelled at the kid.

"The last thing I need is this kid seeing me!" Jane thought. The Silence Protocol applied to North Pole Fae, in addition to Tailors aka tree elves. A human sees you, not only is there imminent danger, there is also the danger of belief in magic diminishing. Human Spirit levels drive the North Pole's very existence. Humans knowing elves, fairies, and Santa exist diminishes the magic considerably. Fairies being seen as common as a house fly would certainly diminish their magic. The whole 'clap if you believe in fairies' pledge is ever important.

Fae had actually been discovered by a human play-wright named J.M. Barrie. His inspiration for Tinker-bell was actually a real, live fairy. However, the leader of the fairies who bring Spring to the world, the Spring Fae, made an agreement with him to keep the fairies' actual existence hidden. Thus, the fictional play 'Peter Pan' had been written and most assuredly would keep the concept of fairies as merely, a child's play fantasy.

The kid who had stopped the revolving door just laughed at her parents' protests and stern looks.

The revolving door seemed to take forever to open

to the lobby. Jane quickly eyed a grand chandelier she could take cover in as long as the kid delighted in the trouble she was in.

"Hahahahaha!" The little brown-haired girl with a puffy jacket cackled.

Jane shook her head and mouthed to herself, "Don't look up. Don't look up."

FOURTEEN
DRYER DIRE

The smallest sliver of space opened to the lobby and Jane shot up and out to the chandelier.

"Phew." Jane delighted in the warm air of the lobby and the heat from the chandelier's lights. She looked to the marble floor and the walls for a sign for a bathroom with a hand dryer. Next to the registration desk were the bathrooms. Jane quickly flew into the women's bathroom after a girl exited. She scanned the bathroom. No one was in the stalls and no one at the sink. Finally, a respite from the constant threat. Jane hovered near the push-activated dryer then charged the button in a drop kick pose. Her first kick started the hot air.

Jane's headache did not improve with the heated dry air. She moved underneath the air spout. The warmed air comforted her wings and body but played hell with her head. Her pants felt drier, her leather jacket would take a bit more time. She didn't know how much more she could take.

The Fae officer flitted away from the dryer to remove her boots then flew back to dry her feet and at least, help the boots get dry. Jane removed the communication device from her ear. Maybe the warm air would get it back to a functioning state. She needed to get a hold of Lily. The nature of Coco's disappearance and how the Tailors described the other missing Fae were too similar to be coincidental.

The dryer stopped its cycle. Jane popped the com back in her ear and lifted her boots. She flapped her achy wings fast enough to push the door open. She headed back to the chandelier and resting on a candelabra, put her boots back on.

"Much better." Jane said to herself rubbing her hands together in comfort from her newly dry state.

She observed a befuddled hotel employee examine the bathroom door probably wondering how the door opened by itself.

She smiled then tapped the com in her ear.

This time some static. Progress.

She tapped it again.

More static. Then a voice crackled.

"Jane. Over."

Jane flapped off the candelabra in excitement.

"Lily! Is that you?'"

"Yes, yes it's me. Your shuttle's beacon went dark over five hours ago. You two okay?" Lily asked in a controlled manner that belied her demeanor as a Communications Tailor.

"To be honest. I could be better. The shuttle was attacked by an eagle. We almost drowned. Then I was abducted by the same eagle that demolished our shuttle when Coco was able to save me but then she disappeared in the same way that the other fairies were in D.C.." Jane stopped to catch a breath.

"So, Coco is missing, along with other fairies?" Lily asked, her voice tinged with worry.

"Yes, oh right, I didn't tell you. Well, consider yourself in the know now. A blur carried her away and I tried to follow but it was no use. The Tailors said the other fairies disappeared in a flash. This was the same thing, except I was close to it and it could have been another fairy using the power Frenetic."

"So fellow Fae abducting other Fae? To what end?"

"I don't actually know if it was a fairy but what the heck else could have grabbed her?"

"Okay, I will do some research on high-speed creatures that could do something like this and get back to you. What is your next move, Jane?"

"I will make my way to D.C. somehow and follow the leads we had. Hit the White House. In the mean-

49

time, I need you to dig up dirt on these Tailor teams led by Cory, Julia, and Will. Someone tipped whoever abducted those other Fae that we were coming. Let's keep all of this between you and me. They had to be tracking our shuttle or following us. Someone at the Pole is a mole."

FIFTEEN

FLYING COACH

Jane sat on the chandelier. She flapped her wings at different speeds. The pain shot back and forth from her shoulder blades to the tips of her wings. There was no way she was going to make it down to D.C. in the state she was in. Battles against the Spiritless elves, dangerous recon missions from the North to the South Pole, tangling with a bloodthirsty eagle weakened her wings. The shorter journeys in short bursts she could take. A long journey from upstate New York to D.C. she could not.

Jane flew back outside of the hotel through bell services' double doors that she found on the side of the building behind the front desk. She hovered underneath the grand awning and listened to a couple waiting for a cab with their luggage.

"This was a nice trip John. Thanks love." The

older woman in a fur coat leaned her head on her husband's shoulder.

"I love you. I wanted our 30th anniversary to be special and what better way to spend it than looking at a wonder of the world with the woman I think is even more beautiful?" The man put his arm around his wife.

Jane hovered above and didn't know if she should gag or cry from the sweetness this couple showed each other. She thought about Brendan and how he was so eager to be in love and start a life together. She had so much she wanted to accomplish first. She knew Brendan was a great elf and partner, but she just couldn't wholly give of herself yet.

"Here's our cab!" The husband waved down the yellow taxi.

The cab rolled up and the driver popped out to grab their luggage. "Heading back to the airport?"

"Yes sir. Thanks!" The couple hopped in the back of the cab.

Jane sprang into action and flew down behind the driver who was lifting the bags into the trunk. The driver rested his hand on the open trunk door then began to push down. Jane's heart beat pounded as she quickly flew into the trunk before the driver shut it.

In the trunk, Jane heard the muffled voices of the couple. She couldn't see much of anything. The darkness of the cab helped her headache. She lay on the leather luggage and let herself rest for a few moments. She shut her eyes and tried to push back the anxiety of Coco and the other Fae's disappearance. Her sedentary state caused stress to increase. Her body was tired, but her mind still raced.

She sat up and then decided to use her wing's lumens. The darkness of the cab's trunk blighted by her magical wings. Jane's wing gave off a yellow-gold light. She examined the luggage tags and couldn't believe her luck.

This bag would be headed towards Alexandria, Virginia. A town close to Washington D.C..

Jane made short work of the zipper and tied her scarf to it to pull it closed. The clothes smelled like booze and chlorine, but she could handle it as she hitched a ride to Washington National Airport, giving her wings much needed rest.

SIXTEEN
LILY P.I.

Lily pushed back from her desk in her ornament home and sighed. She had a ton to do but a friend needed her help. She still had to write debrief reports from the Spiritless invasion a few days ago. She shook off the stress and got right back to work. Lily was less affected by crises since the Christmas of '87 when the Spiritless attempted to steal the Secret Snowball, the device that slows time to allow Santa to deliver presents to the world. She had learned to embrace the cutting nature of decision-making that could render unimaginable consequences. She led her Tailor team when her Captain went missing.

Jane and Coco's current quagmire three years ago would have rattled Lily. Not today. Not now. Too much experience with evil and aggression. The only way to prevail is to fight back but fight better. Be better than those who seek to do harm.

It was time again to be better and fight. Tree elves, like Lily, and fairies like Jane and Coco, are connected and allied in the magical ecosystem of the North Pole. A place that stands for good and selflessness. A place of hope and love. A place that acts as the secret beacon of ideals to a world of life that seems constantly at odds with each other. Lily feared that her investigation of Tailors would shatter the idealism of the North Pole.

Lily wrote the names of the three Tailor Captains Jane mentioned on a pad of paper on her desk. She remembered Captain Cory from the Tailor academy; they had been in the same class. Seemed like a good elf.

It pained Lily that she now had to question her fellow Tailor's character. No elves were perfect. A utopia, the North Pole is not. Close to it, but still no perfection. The Home Tree does have a police department for a reason. They aren't very busy, but they exist.

The other two Captains she would have to do a bit more digging to assess their integrity. They were Tailor Captains so that had to be dignified to a certain degree. Still Jane thinks someone in the North Pole knows something about the disappearances.

Lily powered on her computer. Since she was an active duty Icicle Pilot and Communications Tailor, she had administrative access to every Tailor profile and training logs. She did a search for Captain Cory, nothing major popped up. Her past impression of him wasn't wrong. No write-ups, mostly commendations for service and that he should be placed in an accelerated program at the Academy. Cory looked like a true-blue hero. A talented Captain.

Lily moved on to the next captain, Julia. Nothing major populated. She didn't have the talent Cory had but Julia had a solid record of achievement. However, she dropped out of the academy for a year then re-enrolled. Why the year gap? Lily wrote it down on her pad.

Finally, she searched for anything on Captain Will. Again, nothing much. There wasn't any indication of any foul play in their career history.

The Pilot and Communications Tailor brought up the mission logs and reports of the Fae disappearances. All the same situation. All reported an air capture and then their fairy was gone. However, after the disappearance, Captain Cory reported a much more thorough and prolonged search for his fairy than the other two Captains. Will's crew searched the second longest, and Julia's crew didn't bother to search long at all. Now the searches conducted were only done within their trees and were a long shot but still, Julia was either the smartest Tailor in the situation and saw a tree search as futile or there was something more to it. Lily would make her way to Julia's home ornament. The year's absence from the Academy and her behavior after the disappearance were enough to warrant further investigation.

SEVENTEEN
THE BUTTERED RUMMY

Lily looked at her watch. It was getting late in the NP, 9pm. She shook off the time and went to work. She left her very neat, pristine, and organized ornament on the western residential tree that flanked the Home Tree and headed to the end of her branch for her GiftBox Car. It was nothing fancy. It was small similar in size to a human necklace case. She opened the clamshell case and hopped in. She pulled the starter ribbon and the top of the box closed.

Lily headed to the North Tree where Julia resided. Traffic on the PolAirWay was light. She would be at the Julia's place momentarily. Snow fell into the high beams of Lily's GiftBox car, but it wasn't strong enough to obscure her view. Lily looked at her GlimmerHack's screen that she placed on the passenger seat, it showed Julia's address on branch 5.

Lily flew her vehicle through the down markers that noted the exit for the North Tree's branch and local PolAirWay routes.

Lily made her way down to branch 5. She parked on the end that Julia's home ornament hanged. Lily's heart began to beat slightly faster. She still maintained a cool demeanor as she admired the blue and yellow lights of the North Tree. Julia's ornament was blue and gold, the colors of the North Tree, and a symbol of pride for all those who lived here. It was round, sparkly, and deceivingly bigger upon closer inspection. Lily knocked on the ornament.

The curved door opened right away. "May I help you?" An older, short-haired, female tree elf greeted her. She had dark brown eyes like Lily's mother.

The Pilot and Communications Tailor's glasses had fogged up when the heat from the ornament smacked up against the cold air outside. Lily removed her glasses and wiped them with her sleeve.

"Hello, I was wondering if Julia was around. I just wanted to talk with her I am a fellow Tailor." Lily put her glasses back on.

"Oh, Julia isn't here right now. I believe she said she was going to the bar with her and her friends. They usually head to The Buttered Rummy on the top branch. Can I give her a message for you?" Julia's presumed mother asked.

59

"I actually will head up there now. Thank you very much." Lily turned to leave.

"Okay hon, thanks for stopping by!" She closed the door.

Lily shook her head. She hadn't realized that Julia was young enough to still live with her parents or perhaps her Mom lives with her. She was a new Captain and did apply directly to officer school after the Academy. Lily walked further into the interior of the North Tree and headed to the trunk lift. She pushed the bark button to the right of the lift door and waited. The bark rolled open and the lift was empty. Lily hit the button for the top branch.

The top branch, technically wasn't the tip top of the tree but it was the last branch that ornaments could hang from safely. Lily disembarked and to the right of the lift was The Buttered Rummy. It was a big ornament that resembled a coffee mug spilling over with well, fake buttered rum. The entrance was in the fake bubbles spewing forth from the mouth of the mug.

Lily entered. Inside the huge mug was a long bar to the right and a series of wooden tables; some with green felt for playing cards, some were high tops, and some low seating areas. The ceiling was high and there were dimmed blue and gold lights everywhere. Lily being a West Tree elf, missed the orange and red motif of her home. She was in rival territory.

EIGHTEEN
BAR BRAWL

Cocoa spice was being sold for only one shaving tonight. Cheap Spice, which explained the crowd. Lily scanned the seating areas first then the bar. She walked deeper into the cylindrical bar. No Julia yet. Lily stayed away from the bars in general. She was too busy refining her skills and being 29, this scene made even less sense to her.

She made it to the end of the bar then turned around. A few inches down the bar, a female tree elf had her hair down which was different from the look Lily found in Julia's file. It was ash blonde and hit her shoulders. The female was Julia with her hair down. She talked to another male elf, then Lily quickly realized it was Cory.

"Hey Cory!" Lily walked over to her fellow Academy classmate.

Cory removed his elbows from the bar and looked behind to find the voice that called for him.

"Cory, it's me Lily!" Lily moved closer to Cory.

"Oh, hey! How are you, Lily? The valedictorian at The Buttered Rummy! Wow!" Cory gave Lily a hug. Lily had no choice but to hug back. The smell of the spice on his breath was overwhelming. Lily's brow furrowed.

"Oh hey, this is Julia, a fellow Tailor Captain!" Cory let go of Lily and put his arm around Julia.

Lily put her hand out to shake Julia's hand.

Julia glanced at Lily's hand but did not reach out, "Hey, so you two went to the Academy together?"

Lily could feel Julia's jealousy spewing forth from the tone of her voice and the half-drunk gaze.

"We did graduate the same year. What year did you graduate?"

Julia put her head on Cory's shoulder.

"I took a year off..." Julia jolted forward and fell in front of Cory and at the feet of Lily. Cory turned around to see what caused her fall.

A bigger elf had pushed a smaller elf into Julia's back. Cory in a flash confronted the larger elf.

"What is your problem?"

"Hey man, did not mean to push that East Tree snob into you. Get out of my face before I plant your ass next." The big elf smirked while looking down at

Cory, who was average size and not quite up to the task of having any business facing down the much stronger elf.

Lily helped Julia up. "You okay?"

"I am okay. Oh no, what is Cory doing?" Julia pointed as Cory's right fist raked the jaw of the large, aggressive elf.

The big elf shook off the punch and laughed. He then drove his fist into Cory's stomach. Cory cowered and fell to the ground. The smaller elf who knocked into Julia smashed a Cocoa Spice mug over the large elf's head. Blood trickled down his face.

The smaller elf screamed from being lifted over the head of his opponent then thrown over the bar. Not soon after, the patrons down the bar began to get involved. Soon the localized debacle spread to a bar-wide cataclysm. Lily grabbed Julia's hand.

"We should leave," Lily said.

Julia was flustered from the sudden brawl. Chairs flew through the air, glass shards sprayed into the air along with the loosed Cocoa Spice. Some elves fought for the fun of it. Some legitimately wanted to hurt each other. It was madness.

"What about Cory?" Julia looked back as Lily pulled at her arm.

"He is a big boy elf. He will find his way out of here."

They reached the faux foam door and exited onto the top branch.

The Home Tree Police sirens sounded from the lower branches.

"Let's get you home." Lily felt a need to take care of Julia in her drunken state. She also needed some questions answered.

NINETEEN
WALKY TALKY

"I can wait out here for Cory. I am sure he can take me home."

A group of Home Tree Police ran past the two ladies and entered The Buttered Rummy.

"Do you really want to wait for him now? Might be a while. I am sure he will call you later," Lily said.

Julia stared at the building and sighed then stumbled. She was not fit to make proper decisions. Lily grabbed her to prevent yet another fall.

"You are right. Let's get outta here. What am I even doing? Ha! I can't even stand." Julia stumbled

Lily rolled her eyes. This situation was ridiculous. Taking care of drunk elves was not part of the plan. Lily was never really into the bar scene. Lily sensed that Julia was jealous towards her. It could just be the effects of the spice, but Lily was not attracted to Cory. Julia had nothing to worry about.

"Where are we going?" Lily smiled.

"Branch 5. My ornament is down there. Not far just a short trunk lift ride down." Julia and Lily walked towards the trunk of the North Tree. Lily didn't have much time to ask her questions since Julia's ornament home was close. The spice still flowed through Julia's veins to Lily's advantage.

"You said you took a year off from the Academy? Is that what you said before you were knocked to the ground?" Lily asked.

"Yes, yes, I did. I graduated about five years after you and Cory. I had to take a year off to take care of my Dad." Lily watched as Julia took careful steps looking down at her feet the whole way to the trunk lift.

"Oh no, I am sorry to hear that. He okay now?" Lily couldn't think of anything malicious in Julia's explanation. A dead end.

The bark door to the elevator opened.

"He has a rare disease that causes slow paralysis. Over time he has lost his ability to move. The Home Tree doctors can't cure him. With all the magic of the North Pole, one would think there would be a way." Julia's voice held a tinge of anger mixed with sadness.

"There may still be a way. You never know." Lily stepped into the lift and pushed 5.

"I finally hired a nurse to live with us and she helps with his condition. My Dad wanted me to finish school. I did and now I am a Captain. He is at least comfortable for now. This is my branch. I can make my way home from here. Thanks Lily."

Lily didn't want Julia to know she parked her GiftBox Car on her branch. She debated asking about the missing Fae and Julia's brief report. The lift door began to close after Julia stepped off. Lily stuck her foot in the door causing the door to open again.

"Oh, I meant to ask you and Cory... I mean to say I am a Communications Tailor. I happened to see the missing Fae reports when I was writing up a debrief from a recent mission this year. That was crazy, huh?"

Julia turned around and cocked her head. "Yeah it was weird. That is in the Fairy Fleet's hands now. It's a shame. I grew very close to our Fairy, Molly. I keep tabs on the situation with Pixie. He sent a couple fairies to investigate, but I am not even sure I am supposed to talk about it. That is part of the reason Cory and I get drunk tonight... from the worry."

"Oh, okay, you don't have to say anymore. I just hope all will be well. Good night." Lily could sense Julia's impatience, but still her reaction the Fae query seemed genuine.

Lily stepped back on to the lift and waved. She still

wanted to talk to Cory and ask him a few more questions. These Tailor captains were still her best leads.

TWENTY
D.C.

The flight to D.C. went by quickly for Jane. She shook the sleep from her wings and left the suitcase before she was transported to baggage claim. She pulled at the scarf and opened the suitcase. The luggage tram zipped towards Washington National's terminal. She was happy to have had the rest. It was much-needed. She was so tired that the anxiety of Coco and the other missing Fae couldn't even keep her awake. As soon as she hit the cool D.C. air, however, mission-mode kicked back in. Her headache had subsided for now. She tapped the com in her ear.

"Lily. Over." Nothing.

"Lily, you there? Over."

"Yes, yes, sorry." Lily's voice came through Jane's earbud.

"Any leads over there?"

"As of now. No, I asked Captain Julia a few questions, but she seemed to check out. I still have to ask Cory and Will. Found something interesting. Julia's report on the missing Fae was much shorter than the other two Captains. She was stationed at the Press Club. I asked her a few questions, but she seemed genuinely concerned about the Fae's welfare."

"Hmm... so nothing over there yet. I will head to the White House now since that was the site of the first disappearance. I will keep you updated and I will attach the candy cane, so you can hack in."

"Be mindful of the radar and infrared aka heat sensors for early detection of any missiles, flying objects, etc. Technically, you are in a no-fly zone, Fairy Flyer. Those are stationed on the roof. Although you are so small one would think the heat sensors would ignore you. Nevertheless, proceed with caution."

"Okay thanks Lil'. Talk to you later."

Jane flew near the National Mall. The Washington monument pierced the late-morning sky. The US Capitol building lay in the distance. Jane spotted the White House and flew toward 1600 Pennsylvania. The usual group of protesters that frequented the front gate were doing the usual chanting and walking. The lawn looked impeccably green even in the winter.

Jane planned out her course of action.

There were two Secret Service agents on the roof.

She could easily approach the building without the human seeing her, no matter what high tech equipment they had. The sensitivity levels of the sensors were probably amplified, but not insane enough to single out birds.

Jane slowed her flight speed to that of a robin's, though Jane was smaller than the common bird. Hopefully her theory would prove correct. Jane continued along her flight path to one of the most secure buildings on the planet.

TWENTY-ONE
APPROACH

Jane approached the roof of the White House from the West. The West Wing loomed ahead. She kept a course at the same height as the roof. The flag waved from atop the tall pole. She was over the West Lawn.

The Secret Service agent shifted his view. He looked through the binoculars in the same general direction as Jane.

"Shoot." Jane dropped lower out of his field of vision.

Perhaps the sensors did pick her heat signature up. Another Secret Service agent moved over the West side of the roof to examine the skies.

Jane stopped and hovered. She shook her head.

She couldn't approach without setting off the alarms. She could ignore and continue, but at the risk of raising the security and capture. Her evasion and agility skills were top notch, but she didn't want to take on the Secret Service. Yet.

There were still two other sites to examine. The National Press Club had to be an easier entry.

Jane turned around. "Lily there is no way I can approach the White House without setting off their security measures. I will head to the National Press Club. That should be a piece of cake to infiltrate. Over."

"That will be fine. I will see if I can think of a workaround," Lily said, audibly typing in the background.

"Yes, I think I may have a way. I will let you know. Give me the coordinates of the National Press Club and I will head there next."

"Got them. 529 14th Street NW. Over."

"Oh my. It's down the darn street. Talk soon. Out."

Jane flew to the National Press Club, an almost century-old institution where journalists meet and support each other. Luminaries speak their weekly, sometimes daily. Student groups visit it. Teacher groups visit the Club. It is a D.C. attraction in and of itself.

Jane examined the rooftop. There were no sharp-shooters on post here. She could breathe a bit easier.

She approached the antenna on the rooftop of the

73

building and laid the candy cane signal amplifier at the base.

"Lily. Over." Jane tapped her ear.

"I see you activated your first amplifier. This is very exciting for me actually! I have my GlimmerHack ready and I am receiving a signal! Yes! Okay we just need you to get in there to play the tape from Dec 25th." The volume of Lily's voice raised to match her excitement.

"Lily, it's nice to hear you excited! Usually you're so steely and reserved." Jane smiled as she flew into the raised and curved duct that led into the building.

"Well, it just great that I can actually see the CCTV feed itself with the amplifier. Anywhere there is a camera which looked like every floor of the building and corner. I can see. Let me filter through and direct you to main security hub where they keep the recordings."

Jane flew down the vents. The air warmed as she pushed further into the interior of the National Press Club's ductwork. She was in the central vertical corridor and passed various floors of the building. The Fairy Flyer slowed her descent to wait for Lily.

"Okay as I thought...it's on the first floor near the front entrance. There is a hallway with a bathroom in it and a closed door. Behind that door is the security room. I just saw a guard walk out of it. There should be a corresponding duct for that room. Should be a cakewalk."

"Okay headed down faster now." Jane dove head-first and tucked her wings when she reached the bottom she spread her wings to slow her descent. The maneuver hurt her wings even with the rest they got from the airplane ride.

"When you reach the bottom of the vertical corridor head down the left vent and follow until you see the slits for the security room underneath you."

"Roger that. Heading left."

TWENTY-TWO
VHS

Jane scanned the vent floor below her. Up ahead light from the security room illuminated the dust floating around in the ventilation system.

"Approaching the room now." Jane whispered as to not arouse any suspicion from possible guards on monitor duty.

Jane made it to the slotted vent cover. She landed and looked down. There was a wall of 8-inch monitors that showed the closed circuit television network of every hallway and room in the Club. A guard sat hunched over a cup of coffee. He rubbed his eyes, yawned, and sipped from his reindeer mug.

"Okay Lil' we have a guard at the desk who is staring at the monitors. I can take care of him." Jane whispered.

"How exactly do you plan on doing that?" Lily asked. Jane could sense her restrained cynicism.

"I am a fairy you know. I have a few tricks up my sleeve." Jane opened her bomber jacket and pulled a packet from her interior breast pocket.

Jane slipped through the open slots of the vent cover and hovered over the exhausted security guard. She was sure to flap her wings in a controlled manner. Stealth mode.

She waited for the opportune moment. The security guard again yawned and rubbed his eyes with his right hand; his left remained on the mug.

Jane flew with lightning-quick speed and dropped the packet into his coffee.

She then retreated back to the safety of the ductwork.

The security guard shook his head, yawned again, stood up, walked to the corner, poured more coffee into his reindeer mug. Took a sip.

"Wait for it Lily. You can see this right? Over." Jane asked.

"Yes, there is a cam in this room too. Oh, dear!"

The security guard laid on the floor and curled up in a fetal position. The heavy breathing of deep sleep resonated through the room.

"DUST has a lot of different uses, Lily. One of

which is security precautions in case a human sees us on missions. Knock 'em out." Jane laughed.

"Brilliant. For how long?" Lily asked.

"I gave him the whole packet. We have enough time 'til the other guards switch duties for sure."

"Excellent work, Jane. Now see that larger monitor to the right of the wall of smaller monitors? That is the surveillance review television. The that tower next to it is several Video Cassette Recorders. They can record hours of footage. The tapes from earlier this week should still be available in the players and not archived."

Jane flew down into the security office. She looked at the larger television and next to it and saw the Video Cassette Recorder tower.

"There are labels of the days and rooms on each VCR. This was a Christmas Day Lobby abduction. Here it is." Jane looked over at the sleeping security guard. His coffee spilled and began to drip on the floor. She flitted her wings then pushed the play button on the VCR. She flew back to watch.

"Lily, can you see the footage?"

"I can but it is not very big on the screen. I am recording I should be able to zoom in and clean up the footage with my GlimmerHack later. In the meantime, you should fast forward 'til about 6am. Will's report said the incident occurred in that hour," Lily said.

"Got it. I am assuming it's the button with the arrows that point right?" Jane flew to the VCR's fast forward button. She looked over at the TV for the countdown to 0600. The tape took a while to get there. Jane hovered and kept pressure on the button. She stopped it at 0558.

The screen showed a security guard staring at the Christmas tree and checking his watch then the guard walked away. As soon as the guard walked away the fairy emerged from the tree. The Tailors were doing their morning checks right on time with assistance of the Fairy Flyer. The fairy flitted around the tree for a while stopping at certain areas of the tree and pointing. The recording was not very clear, Jane could tell what was happening. Then it happened.

The fairy disappeared.

"Ah crap Lily! I missed it. What do I do with this thing?"

"Rewind the tape and intermittently pause it. Then examine the screen."

"Ugh arrows pointing left I presume." Jane pushed the rewind button and looked at the screen. The security guard snorted. He started drooling on the floor. Next to his spilled coffee cup was a remote control.

"Lily why didn't you tell me there was a remote!" Jane flew over to the desk and used her feet to push the buttons. Much easier.

"Sorry Jane. I didn't realize that. You might want to hurry up in there. I checked the lobby camera and a guard is headed your direction. I will keep you updated."

Jane didn't ignore Lily's comment, but she kept focus on the tape. She kept playing and pausing the tape.

"There!" Jane flew closer to the screen to examine the disappearance and determine a point of contact. Nothing showed on the screen. The area around the missing Fae was clear. Near the base of the tree was a strange blip. It looked like another fairy. Jane looked closer.

"Lily, I think I have something."

"Jane, you don't have much time. The guard is about to open...wait he stopped and went into the bathroom instead. Phew. What do you got?"

"It can't be..." Jane's mouth dropped. She flew back to the desk and pushed play on the remote. The fairy disappeared. Then she paused again.

Jane examined the screen. The blip or fairy near the base of the tree was still there. Part of her was relieved but not completely satisfied. Jane' eyes were open wide. She shook her head.

"Jane. You need to move now!" Lily yelled.

Jane flew quickly up to the vent. The guard entered the room.

"Hey Bobby! What the heck 'a ya doin'? Wake up!" The guard scolded the unconscious guard and shook his shoulder.

Jane slipped through the vent cover.

"Lily." Jane was careful to whisper.

"You see anything?"

"I did. I think I need to pay a visit to my sister. Now."

TWENTY-THREE

SOLSTICE FAE

Jane headed to the central shaft that would lead her up and out the National Press Club.

"Your sister?" Lily typed audibly in the background.

"Yes. My sister. What are you doing?" Jane flew fast. Her emotions were all over the place. She was mad, anxious, concerned, and disappointed all at the same time.

"I am converting the footage to a digital file to zoom in to what you saw in greater detail. Why your sister?"

"She left the Pole a few years back. She is a Solstice Fae. She would be busy this time of year on this side of the globe. Bringing winter to the US. I saw a Solstice Fae near the base of the tree at the same time as the disappearance, except it was still there after our Fae Flyer disappeared. Whatever that means. Last time I checked up on her she was stationed in D.C." Jane reached the rooftop of the National Press Club.

"Okay I can see it. How could you tell it was a Solstice Fae? Oh wait, never mind. They glow at this time of year."

"Yes, in season they glow when they use their DUST to spread winter. Snow fall is actually caused by the Solstice Fae as cover to keep doing their work, which begs the question: what would that type of Fae be doing inside of a building at this time of year?" Jane asked while resting her wings on the roof.

"Maybe they were part of the abduction or investigating it themselves? There is no mention of any Solstice Fae on any of the Tailor Captain's reports. There is a hollow of Solstice Fae located on the Potomac, Theodore Roosevelt Island, not far from the National Mall. Head west to George Washington Memorial Parkway. You can't miss it. I will examine the footage to see if I can see anything else."

"I will head there now." Jane's wings still ached. Every time she stopped then started, she went through the same painful process of getting used to the soreness again and again. Her head still felt good. Although the stress of having to see her sister already sent a wave of pain to her temples.

Her sister had left NP Hollow five years ago to follow her own path, even though their parents wanted her to follow in their footsteps. There was always a certain degree of tension between the Jane and her well before she left. It had been a while since Jane saw her sister in any situation, let alone a situation as dire as the one she and her fellow Flyers were in now.

The flight was short. The island was almost as wide as the Potomac itself. It served as a living memorial to one of the United States' most gregarious and hearty Presidents. Much of Faedom owes the preservation of their Hollows in the United States to Theodore Roosevelt's National Park Service.

There was an old tree in the center of the island that looked secluded and appropriate for a Hollow. Jane flew down to the winter-bitten island. Her heart beat faster in anticipation.

She flew to the base of the tree.

"Stop. Do not come any closer." A voice burst from the tree trunk.

"I am here to see Kath. I am her sister, Jane. Is she here?"

A root emerged from the frozen ground and a door opened on it.

"I take it I can come in? Am I supposed to climb in to the root?"

"Yes. Don't be an idiot."

Jane knew it was Katherine.

"Kath. Already spewing insults." Jane flew into the

root. The root was dark, and she could feel immense air pressure pulling her in as if she was stuck in a huge vacuum. Jane had no control. The air warmed the further she spiraled through the tube. She dropped into a bed of feathers. The Hollow was lit neon blue and green. The lighting flickered. There were many tunnel openings leading up the tree. Jane lay still on the feathers before she took off her aviator helmet, exasperated.

"Kath! That was not cool. How about a warning?" She yelled. A few Solstice Fae emerged from the tunnels at various heights of the Hollow.

"You, being here is alarming enough." Behind Jane was her dark-haired, shorter sister who held out her hand.

TWENTY-FOUR
PHANTOMS

Lily perused the footage a few more minutes. The same thing over and over. The Fairy Flyer just vanishes. It was almost noon. She still had to ask a few more questions of Cory. She hoped that by now he would have recovered from his Cocoa Spice hangover and whatever injuries he had sustained in the bar fight. She dialed his number rather than leave her ornament.

The phone rang several times. Lily remained patient.

"Yello."

"Cory, it's Lily. Did you make it out of there okay last night? Police shut the Rummy down or what?" Lily asked.

"Oh yeah, I got out of there not long after you two left. That was insane. I am a little sore but okay. How are you? Thanks for getting Julia home by the way. I really appreciate it. How can I help you? Two days in a row I hear from the top of my class." Cory's voice turned from raspy to smooth the more he talked.

"I am good. I will be honest. I have a few questions about the missing Fae. I am helping out the investigation and need a few details from you," Lily said.

"Oh wow. I thought that was the Fleet's issue now."

"Yes, it is. I am helping out of one the investigators. I just have a few questions. Do you mind?"

"No, no. Not at all. I wanted to do more but Pixie insisted he and the Fleet would handle it. I left a pretty detailed report." Cory was fully awake now.

"Your report is very detailed, and I thank you for that. I just wanted to know why Julia's report was brief. Maybe you might have some insight on that?" Lily plowed ahead. Time for sensitivities was at an end.

"Oh, that is odd. No, I don't have any reason why she wouldn't have left more detail. I mean there is no rule against lack of detail on the reports. I mean she is going through a lot. Her Dad is sick. When she is home she has to help him and relieve the nurse they hire. She probably just rushed through it to get home." Cory came to Julia's defense quickly.

"Yes, she told me about her Dad. Okay, I just thought I should ask. We are just having a hard time finding any leads and her brief report stood out is all. If you think of anything that you forgot to report just drop me a line. Okay?" Lily asked.

"Sure thing, Lily. Same thing goes for you." Cory ended the call.

JANE GRABBED her sister's hand. Kath pulled her up.

"Are you missing Fae too?" Kath asked.

"Yes. Yes. Actually." Jane had a hard time transitioning to business so quickly.

"We are missing Fae as well. It started about a week ago." Kath turned and walked away.

Jane quickened her pace. "You haven't even said hello yet. Right to business."

"Spare me the sentimentality. You are only here because you need something. That is the only time you have ever interacted with me. Need a shirt to wear you used to raid my room. The list goes on," Kath said.

"Now wait a minute, we both borrowed each other's clothes." Jane was wrapped up in her sister's usual bluntness.

"Yes, until you grew taller than me. Now what do you know? You share first. Fairies have gone missing." Kath turned to look at her sister.

Jane was flabbergasted.

"Kathy, stop. You are so much smart— "

"What did I say? Let's leave our sibling rivalry out of this. Spare the sentiment. We have to move fast. I have my Fae out searching and finishing the transition from Fall to Winter at the same time. The disappearances are not untraceable. We have found DUST remnants."

Jane shook her head and accepted her sisters will to brush past their problems again.

"What about the remnants? Anything unique?" Jane asked.

"They pulse between a visible and invisible state. What do you have for me? How did you know to come find us in the first place?" Kath crossed her arms.

"We are missing four Fairy Flyers, one of whom is my good friend Coco. We have locations of where they went missing and a timeline. The National Press Club, were you there?"

"Yes, I was there on Christmas Day. I followed a trail of the disappearing DUST. How did you know I was there? Stalker."

"No, I was able to see you on the footage from the surveillance cameras."

"Novel idea, to use the human's camera system. Anything else on the footage that would be helpful?"

"No, but my friend Lily is analyzing it as we speak."

LILY OUTSTRETCHED her arms over her head and let out a big yawn. The footage bore nothing new. The best footage would most likely be from the White House recordings. The President's home would most assuredly have better quality surveillance systems than the Press Club.

Lily looked out her ornament. The hairs on the back of her elven neck stood up. She looked out her window. There was nothing out there, but her wonderful view of the Home Tree. Still, something didn't feel right. Lily noticed the light fixture above her desk moved ever so slightly and swung back and forth. She stared at it until it stopped swinging.

The sensation of falling overwhelmed Lily. Her stomach leapt to her throat. Her ornament, her home was falling down her tree. Lily grabbed for her GlimmerHack. It flew up to the ceiling then crashed down. Lily fell over still in her chair. Her ornament had crashed a few branches lower than her home branch.

Lily didn't want to move and cause the ornament to fall further down the tree. Her desk pinned her right foot. She grabbed for her GlimmerHack. She felt a blow to the side of her head. The blood trickled out of her ear. She was too dazed to pinpoint what hit her. Then another hit landed on the side of her head. Lily lay unconscious.

TWENTY-FIVE

STICK AND MOVE

"Who is Lily? Is she Fae?" Kath asked.

"No, she is a tree elf and a great friend. I trust her. She is a heck of an elf. A Communications Tailor who knows her way around high tech more than the two of us." Jane insisted, hoping to diffuse her sister's cynicism.

"So, she can hack into security systems. I can see her usefulness. I had some samples of the DUST we found, they seem to have a short lifespan. They only stay visible for so long before they dissipate completely which makes it harder to trace but again, not impossible." Kath walked away from Jane again.

"Do you have to walk away from me when we are clearly having a conversation?" Jane walked to catch up.

"I am headed to my quarters to show you the phantom DUST. I am just trying to be helpful," Kath said.

"Be helpful in a less annoying way if that is possible for you, which it is not." Jane glared.

The neon blue and green lights of the D.C. Hollow flickered. Then blacked out. The ambient light from outside still provided enough light.

"That's not good." Kath flapped her wings. Jane followed suit.

"Everybody good? Just a power outage is all." Kath scanned the Hollow for any signs of foul play. The sisters Fae looked up to the various tunnels along the roots of the Hollow.

The first scream sounded from above and behind them. Then another on their right side.

"Well I am sure glad you led these darn Phantom Fae here Jane. Thanks a lot." Kath flew in the direction of the first scream. The root tunnel once occupied by a fellow Solstice Fae was empty. Jane had searched the root tunnels the second scream originated from. Nothing.

"Kath! We should stick together! We will be harder to pick off if we stay together!" Jane quickly turned around and headed back to the center of the Hollow.

"Kath! Katherine! Where are you?" Jane scanned

the various tunnel openings up and down the center shaft.

"I got one!" Kath burst out of a tunnel. Her arm was outstretched. She was hanging on to something. She was being dragged by something invisible, a phantom.

Jane chased Kath who was still being dragged but vertically. The phantom was looking for a way out of the Hollow.

"You are going to have to fly faster sister!" Kath looked down at Jane. Kath's grip still held strong but wouldn't last long.

"Hang on!" Jane grimaced. The Power Frenetic was her only way to catch up. Her wings flapped faster, stronger, which sent shooting pain up and down Jane's spine. She had no choice. Jane wing's glowed bright yellow, the Hollow's neon green and blue interior was splashed with a gold streak.

Kath observed her sister catching up. "Don't grab me! Grab the phantom!"

"I know that, Kath!" Jane flew parallel to the virtually empty space above her sister. Jane reached out with her left arm. She felt a punch on her forearm.

"I got you now! Kath get ready to fly."

The shaft's ceiling neared. There were tunnels that split off into the branches of the top of the tree, Jane knew she had to stop the phantom in the shaft between the top tunnels and root tunnels. She may lose the phantom in the branches. The time to act was now.

Jane still utilizing the Power Frenetic flew past Kath and the phantom. She maintained a steady pace above them. The branches were inches away. Jane began her dive with fists clenched and arms out.

She saw Kath twist to the right but the phantom's attempt to dodge Jane failed.

Jane felt as if she was tackling someone in mid-air. The phantom curled from Jane's shoulder implanted into its mid-riff. Kath let go and flitted away.

Jane moved to scrape the phantom off the side of the Hollow. The phantom flashed into a visible mode then back into an invisible state. Jane drove the phantom into the bark of the Hollow and stopped. The pain from the tackle caused the phantom to become visible.

"Kath! Gimme a hand here!"

Kath flew next to Jane. They both hovered and pinned the now-visible phantom to the wall. It wore a steel grey uniform. It had wings. Its face was mostly covered by a mask that only revealed its eyes.

"What are you?" Kath looked closer into its' eyes.

An audible crack echoed off the Hollow's walls. The phantom's head drooped.

"Did this thing's neck just break?" Jane asked.

Kath looked visibly upset. She pulled the mask off the phantom.

"What's wrong?" Jane held back showing her pain from the Power Frenetic.

"This phantom was one of my Fae."

TWENTY-SIX
EXAMINATION

Jane and Kath lay the Solstice Fae turned phantom on the ground near where Jane had entered the Hollow earlier.

A few Solstice Fae had gathered around the dead phantom.

Jane noticed Kath was silent, probably reeling from the phantom's true identity.

"Kath, I know this is a sensitive situation but if we want to prevent something like this from happening again. We have to get back to work," Jane said.

"Jane. A Fae of mine, Sara, is dead and I just need some time to process without you bossing me around." Kath scoured.

"We will have to examine what happened to her and look at all her gear. I will do it. In the meantime, I suggest everyone leave the Hollow immediately." Jane ignored her sister and went into command-mode. Jane bent down to examine the phantom.

"Don't touch her." Kath grabbed her sister's arm.

Jane stood up. "Do you really want to do this now?" Jane used her taller, physical prowess to subtly intimidate Kath. It didn't work.

"Let go of her." Tears visibly welled in Kath's eyelids.

Another Solstice Fae stepped in and broke Kath's grip on Jane's arm.

"Kath, Jane is right. We just lost another fairy. There had to be at least two of the phantoms in here because Yuridia is gone now too. We will take care of Sara here."

Kath backed down and walked a few inches away.

Jane shook her head then bent down again to examine Sara.

Her dark uniform was well constructed. Her wings were painted black. On her spine where her wings met was a square device with a blinking red light.

"This may be a tracker." Jane looked at the square device; it had two wires leading up to Sara's neck.

"This looks like a master control device. This might have been what caused her to break her neck?" Jane said aloud.

"Enough electric shock aimed at a fairy's neck would break it." Kath walked back wiping a tear off her cheek. Kath checked Sara's jacket and pants pockets. More phantom DUST particles.

"That is the same DUST you found before, right?" Jane asked.

"Yes, it is. We have to go. We still have those surveillance feeds you said right?" Kath was now fully composed, or at least as much as she could be.

"Yes, the White House is where I want to go next, but they have infrared sensors that I can't get past without setting off alarms and locking the place down," Jane said.

"Well, infrared sensors detect heat signatures. I happen to be a trained Solstice Fae. I bring winter to the world. I can cool myself down enough to slip right past the heat signatures." Kath smirked.

"Yes, that just might work! Let me check in with Lily." Jane tapped her com.

"Lily?"

No response.

"Lily. Over." Jane waited for a response.

Kath grew impatient. "Jane, we have to move. Call her later."

Jane tried one more time. "I am sure she will get back to me soon."

THE FLUORESCENT TUBE lighting of the hospital

branch was neither inviting nor comforting. Lily looked around. The Tailor medics wheeled her into a room, then a doctor walked in with a chart.

"Oh good. She is conscious. Hey Lillian, I am Doctor Yule. You took a nasty fall and lost consciousness. However, you will be okay." He walked to the right side of her bed.

"Thanks Doctor. I can't quite move my leg. Is it broken?" Lily cut to the chase.

"Unfortunately, we had to put your leg in a brace. It is broken but should heal just fine. We will be in later to put you in a cast."

The medics were still in the room.

"What happened?" Lily asked.

"Your ornament's hook detached from your branch. A freak accident." One of the medics answered.

Lily didn't answer. She could feel the bandaging on her head. Did Julia or Cory try to kill her? Cory seemed upset when she asked about Julia's report. She remembered she felt like someone kicked her in the head twice. Of course, no one in the North Pole would ever think that possible. Nothing seriously bad ever happened here. Until recently, Lily had believed that too.

This was no accident. She had to get a hold of Jane immediately.

The medics were about to leave. Lily stopped them, "Hey, do you guys have my stuff?"

"Yes, it's in your bag which is hanging on the side of your bed." The medics left the room.

Lily reached up to tap her com in her ear. It was gone.

She grabbed for the bag.

Doctor Yule said, "Lily, I suggest you get some rest. Work can wait. You've been through a lot." He smiled then left the room.

Lily ignored him and search through her bag. Her ID and credentials were in the bag. No com. No GlimmerHack. No way to help Jane. Someone wanted the investigation to stop and it would only be a matter of time before someone came to finish her off. Lily needed to get off the hospital branch now, broken leg and all.

TWENTY-SEVEN

WHITE HOUSE

Kath and Jane flew to the perimeter of the President of the United States home.

"I flew towards it and about got halfway over the lawn before the Secret Service agents started getting antsy. So instead of poking the bear I went to the Press Club first."

"This will be a piece of cake. Where do I go when I get in there?" Kath asked.

"I have no idea. I am hoping Lily will get back to us. Here, take this candy cane and put it on the flag pole or one of the antennas up there. It will allow Lily to hack into the system and point you in the right direction."

"Or I can just follow one of the Secret Service agents around 'til I find the security room." Kath took a deep breath and adjusted her gloves and zipped her jacket all the way up.

"That works too," Jane admitted.

"Zip up its about to start snowing again." Kath spun in circles in mid-air like a graceful figure skater jumps. She glowed blue. The skies over the White House started snowing. The huge snowflakes that humans like to catch in their mouths.

Kath stopped spinning. "We will be in touch."

Jane smiled. She was impressed with her sister's wintry abilities to the point of actual pride.

KATH'S TRAINING PAID OFF. She was able to wield nature's power with effortless grace. She was granted her own Solstice Fae Hollow faster than any other fairy ever. She demonstrated excellence and was able to flourish with the Solstice Fae away from the shadow of her sister and her parent's expectations. She knew that she was partially motivated by her younger sister's ability and leadership prowess. It was a blessing and a curse to be in a military family and to constantly compare herself to her sister. It drove her away from the North Pole but also drove her to succeed.

Kath observed the roof of the White House. The Secret Service agents were on duty. They didn't appear to be alarmed. They popped their collars and put on gloves. The heavy snow fall provided Kath cover. The heat sensors were not tripped at all and any motion sensor would be rendered mute by snow.

The roof of the White House had a long rectangular structure that must be the station for the security equipment. Maybe she wouldn't have to go to deep into the building after all. Kath flew to examine it and found an easy way in. There was only one vent and it was large enough for her to enter.

The interior of the rectangular structure was a series of panels, computer equipment, monitors and a few chairs for the agents to sit on. One of the monitors showed various perimeter camera views of the outside of the building. Kath waited for the screen to show interior camera views, but they never came. More alternating view of outside, the lawns, the gates, the back, the front.

"Crap." Kath swore. She would have to penetrate deeper within the White House.

JANE OBSERVED the roof of the White House from beyond the perimeter. She was happy to see that no alarms had been raised nor had the attention of the Secret Service been drawn.

She tapped her com. "Lily. Over."

Static.

"Lily. Over. Again. Can you hear me? Over." Jane didn't know if she should allow her worry to rule her quite yet.

She would try again soon.

TWENTY-EIGHT
ESCAPE

Lily turned to the phone next to her bed. She picked it up. There was no dial tone. The phone was dead. She tapped the nurse call button.

A middle-aged male elf walked in.

"What can I get you? I was just about to come in here actually. The doctor wanted me to give you something for the pain until they can come in and cast your leg."

"My phone is actually dead. Can you help me? I just need to make a call." Lily insisted and pushed herself up to a sitting position.

"That is odd. Yes, let me see what is happening with the phones." The nurse left the room.

Lily needed to move now. She disconnected her IV and threw off her blankets. She swung her braced right leg off the bed then her good leg. She limped to the hallway. The nurse station was empty. It was a low-key day in the Home Tree Hospital ER. She turned back around to grab the pain meds left on the tray in her room. The pain of her broken leg was manageable at the moment, but she would need the meds soon enough.

She limped as fast as she could to the exit door at the end of the hallway before the nurse or anyone could notice. She pushed the door open. A stairwell lay beyond the door. She must have been on the side of the hospital ornament that faced off the tree. There were no doors to the outside.

Lily decided to go down the stairs. She heard footsteps from below. The basement entrance couldn't be too far down. The footfalls were harder and louder. The elf was in a hurry.

Lily risked it and kept waddling down the stairs. The faster she could get out of the hospital the safer she would be and the sooner she could inform Jane of the latest news. She stopped as she saw him. The elf was big. He had a mask on his face and was dressed in black. Lily couldn't believe her luck.

"I get it. The ornament accident failed to kill me, and you are here to finish me off." Lily gripped the railing and stopped in the middle of a flight of stairs.

The masked elf didn't respond. His silence scared Lily more than his presence. He grabbed for Lily's broken and braced leg but missed. Lily fell forward and grabbed his head. Her good knee spiked his face. She didn't let go. She jumped on his back and wrapped and locked her arms around his neck in a chokehold. He staggered back couple steps to the landing and drove Lily's back into the stairwell wall. Lily's head smacked against the wall, but she powered through the brutal blow.

"No!" Lily screamed. She pulled and squeezed harder on his trachea.

"Ack!" The burly, masked elf, fell to his knees.

He pushed himself back to his feet and drove Lily back into the wall again.

She didn't let go. The tears of pain poured down her face, yet she fought harder. The Spiritless threat had hardened her. Lily was no longer just a Pilot and Communications Tailor. She was a warrior.

He fell to the cold stairwell floor immobile.

Lily unlocked her arms. She wasn't sure if he was dead or just unconscious. She pulled the mask off.

She recognized him. It was the elf that helped start the bar fight at The Buttered Rummy. A connection to Captain Cory and Julia, a hired hand of theirs?

His elf phone buzzed. She grabbed it. She kept moving down to the basement. She moved her way through the hospital supply floor and the laundry department and found her way outside and on to the

Home Tree's Hospital Branch. A few other ornament departments hung from the branch. Lily hobbled her way to the center trunk elevator confidently even though she looked like hell. She stopped to tighten her brace and pushed forward. She needed to get to a GlimmerHack or computer as soon as possible.

TWENTY-NINE
JELLY BEANS

Kath flew to a stairwell that lead down into the White House from the rectangular security hub on the roof. She was surprised to see her way rather clear. She made her way to the lobby. The staff was taking ornaments off the tree. Kath hovered close, she still glowed blue. She had remained in her Winter-mode in case the interior had heat sensors as well.

She remembered that the President's main office was in the West Wing. There had to be several Secret Service agents around that she could follow to a hub and the camera recordings. Kath stuck closely to the ceilings above the tilted surveillance cameras. If she needed to pass a camera she would fly as fast as she could.

The walls were white, and the carpet was a navy blue. Kath headed west to the Oval Office. In the hallway to the office, there were a few desks, a receptionist. The place was busy. The typical black suits stood at certain points along the hallway. She heard the crackle of one of the Secret Service agents' ear pieces. The agent then put the earbud in his ear and adjusted his tie.

The President of the United States walked right under Kath and headed to the Oval Office. She seized the opportunity and followed the President.

THE FAE FLYER tapped her com again.

"Lil— "

A voice burst through the earbud. It wasn't Lily.

"Jane. This is Admiral Pixie. Don't be alarmed Lily came to my office and informed you needed more help. Lily had an important meeting with Tailor command for a hearing on the Spiritless invasion."

"Okay sir. Yes, we have run into some difficulty, but we were handling it. I didn't want to inform you until we had something substantial to report." Jane lied. She just thought Pixie was incompetent and didn't want his help, perhaps to a fault. Things, under his watch, had not been going particularly well.

"I am sending Captain Cory and Will to assist you. The Tailor Captains who filed the reports." Pixie's voice seemed forced as if he was uncomfortable.

"Yes sir, I thought we were keeping this a matter for the Fleet, sir?"

"Jane, in light of recent events, the Big Man wants all organizations to work together to combat any threats. They will be in touch when they enter D.C. airspace. They will be in a Tailor Icicle. I am going to give Lily's com over to Cory for now."

Jane heard the shuffle of the transfer to Cory's ear.

"Jane! We are on our way. Looking forward to working with you."

KATH STILL HUGGED the ceiling and kept pace with the President. She had to quickly dive to get through the doorway. No one noticed. The Oval Office was truly oval. The President's desk was at the narrow part of the oval. American flags were stationed around the room on flagpoles. The President sat behind his desk examined his daily agenda before grabbing for jar of jelly beans. It was low.

"Hey Bill, could you get some more jelly beans in here?"

"Right away sir. The bag's in our office." Bill the burly Secret Service agent grabbed the jar off the President's desk.

"You know you can tell a lot about a man if they

choose a specific flavor or just grab a handful, Bill," the President said.

"Good to know Mr. President." Bill smiled and picked up the jelly bean jar.

Kath seized upon the opportunity. She wanted to make sure she made it into the Secret Service office. She dove for open jar of jelly beans as Bill was turning away from the President and took shelter under a black jelly bean. It smelled like licorice. Kath wanted to gag.

Bill waved at the air as if a fly had buzzed his face. He looked around but kept walking. The President needed jelly beans right away.

THIRTY
IREEEEEEENE

Lily didn't want to involve anyone else, but she felt she had no choice. Her ornament had been sabotaged, GlimmerHack stolen, and her com device presumably taken. She had used a closed com in her communication with Jane. It was encrypted so it would be difficult to break into. She saved the password on her Glimmer-Hack, which, again, was gone.

She had to try.

She hobbled to Irene's ornament door. She knocked. No answer. She knocked again.

"Oh, please be home." Lily rubbed the upper of thigh of her broken leg. She needed to rest her leg and keep it elevated for a while.

Irene, the Lighting Tailor, finally opened the door. She and Lily had worked together on a Tailor crew. Irene was best at making sure Christmas lights were functional and working properly. It was an intense job considering how many lights humans put on pine trees. If the lights dry the tree out they can cause fires at times.

"Lily?! What is happening? Get in here!" Irene smiled at first then reacted to Lily's physical and broken appearance. She helped Lily into her ornament, and over to the couch in front of the fireplace. This fireplace only had the illusion of a fire however, no actual fires were allowed on any trees in the North Pole.

"What is going on?" Irene knelt on the floor next to Lily.

"I was helping Jane with a case of three Fae that never returned with their Tailor Teams. The Fleet wanted to handle it, but Jane brought me in to help her with the investigation remotely. So, I did. The fairies ran into some problems. Coco is now missing too, and Jane is still trying to find all of them. Hopefully, she is working with her sister. I was cleaning up some surveillance video we found that showed the abductions when my ornament was sabotaged and thrown from the branch and sent on a terrible rampage down the tree. My leg's broken as you can see and—" Lily stopped when the goon's phone vibrated again. She looked at the number that flashed on the elfphone.

"Irene, do you have a computer or a GlimmerHack or anything like that?"

"Yes, yes I do. I just bought myself this for Christmas." Irene brought over a brand new GlimmerTab, a rectangular flat electronic computer that worked by touch.

"Grab your elfphone cord too." Lily booted up the GlimmerTab. It bore a bigger screen than her GlimmerHack and would do the trick.

"Whose phone is that?" Irene asked giving Lily the cord.

"The goon who tried to kill me at the hospital. I have a feeling I know who is trying to call him. I asked a few questions to the Tailor Captains that reported the Fae missing and I think they don't want me poking around anymore." Lily calmly attached the cord from the phone to the GlimmerTab.

She tapped on the touchscreen quickly and furiously.

Irene just tried to process all the information. It had been a rough holiday season for her as well. She played an integral role in thwarting the Spiritless invasion.

"Got it. I am in." Lily grabbed the goon's phone and opened up to voicemail. She played the last voicemail.

"Where are you? We are leaving without you. Did you take care of it? Ugh...Do I have to send someone else to the hospital? Head to the Icicle

Hangar after it's done, in fact, call me when it's done."

Lily was right. Captain Cory's voice burst through the goon's phone.

"Well, we have some shady Tailors in the North Pole after all." Lily stopped the voicemail. Lily's idealistic and hopeful views of elvenkind took a turn for the worse.

"The voicemail said they were heading to the Icicle Hangar. No Icicle launches are allowed after the Christmas season. How will they pull that off?" Irene asked.

"They must be getting some sort of emergency clearance to launch. Cory has a clean record, so no one would suspect him of foul play. We need to get to the Hangar now! I can't reach Jane with this elfphone but I could possibly break into the closed com we were using with an Icicle's communication system."

Lily grimaced as she tried to get off the couch.

"Do you want something for the pain?"

"Good point. I have some actually." Lily fished the pills the nurse left for her. The pills would help her for a small amount of time anyway.

THIRTY-ONE

FOUND FOOTAGE

Kath, hidden under a licorice jelly bean, could see the wrinkles of Bill, the Secret Service agent's palm, through the glass of the jar. She also was sure to check the ceiling for any doorways that would indicate he was in a new room. He had left the Oval Office and was in the hallway. Another doorjamb appeared, and Bill stopped moving. Kath flapped her wings, pushed the licorice bean off of her, and flew out with incredible speed leaving a cold draft in her wake.

Bill again waved his hand in the air.

"What the?" Bill looked into the jelly bean jar with much consternation. Kath hovered close to the ceiling. She had made it into the security room. The monitors were similar to the ones on the roof, but there were many more. The whole wall was lined with them. Had to be over 100 rooms that were monitored with cameras, Kath needed to find the lobby footage near the Christmas tree.

Bill filled the jar with more jelly beans. "Gotta keep these in here away from POTUS he would eat three bags a day if he could." There was another Secret Service agent eating lunch in the room casually looking at the monitors, who nodded his head. Bill walked out.

Kath hovered near the ceiling then brought out from her blue jacket, DUST she would employ on the hungry agent.

She flew down and strafed the agent, his lunch, and the desk in front of him. His head hit the desk hard.

Kath landed on the desk and rested her wings. She looked for the lobby feed. It had a number on it. Number one actually. Jane told her to look for a play-back device with arrow buttons. She found a small device with only numbers and the arrow buttons on it. Above the numbered control pad was a larger monitor that was not showing any feeds.

This had to be the playback machine.

Kath hit the number one on the keyboard. The lobby feed showed up with a series of chapter numbers. This was different from what Jane described. Kath picked the December 23rd feed. She started her review of the feed from midnight onwards with the fast-forward button. The tree's lights were off. The whole night passed with no incident. A few people shuffled around the tree. A couple tour groups. Then around 3pm the lobby cleared. Staff was setting up for a Christmas gathering. They were done shuffling around at about 6pm.

There was much more action in the feed now at 645 p.m. People entered the lobby and marveled at the pretty tree. Cocktails were served. Around 8pm the guests were moved into a dining area, all except one human who stayed back.

Kath stopped fast forwarding. The man wore glasses and had a beard. He examined the tree thoroughly. He reached into his tuxedo jacket. At first, he pulled out what looked like an ID. He shook his head put the ID back in his pocket and then grabbed a small glass container. He unscrewed the top as if to let something out. Kath flew closer to the screen. It had to be a phantom Fae. She couldn't see the contents of the container, which he closed and then walked out of the lobby.

Kath didn't hesitate. She pulled her elfphone from her pocket with her GlimmerFreeze case on. She rewound the tape and took pics of the man when he brought out his ID.

"Gotcha." Kath smiled.

The agent still slept soundly from the DUST.

It was time for Kath to get back to her sister. She had a solid lead.

THIRTY-TWO
HANGAR HIJINKS

The two tree elves, Lily and Irene, drove to the Icicle Hangar in Irene's GiftBox car. Irene parked the car then helped Lily out. There was an elevator to the Hangar control room. They hopped on.

"If we can take control of the Hangar we can prevent them from launching by shutting the bay doors," Lily said.

"If they haven't launched already," Irene said. Her face stricken with worry.

They entered the Hangar. It was late and empty of elves. Lily limped over to the controls for the bay doors. She pulled at the levers.

"They jammed the controls. They must not be planning a return trip. Stealing an Icicle is career suicide." Lily tried to move a few more levers.

The screen above the window turned on. The launch countdown started.

"Shoot." Irene covered her mouth.

"Well, now we have no choice. We have to follow them." Lily started back towards the elevator.

Irene viewed a standard Icicle ship launch out of the vast Hangar bay.

"Ready, Irene? Brendan's Icicle is in Bay 22. Let's head there now. An Icicle is our only chance at chasing them and warning Jane."

"Should we call Brendan or someone for help?" Irene asked.

"There isn't time. We have to handle this ourselves and even I am not supposed to be part of this mission. She brought me in to help in secret," Lily answered.

Irene joined Lily on the elevator. They used Irene's car and drove to Bay 22 passing row after row of Icicle ships all parked vertically in their bays, awaiting maintenance and drills in preparation for next year's Christmas season.

The superstructure that ran up the side the of Icicle ship didn't have an elevator. Only steps, clearly a design flaw. Most Tailors just used their GlimmerLifts to ascend to the top. Lily and Irene didn't have theirs.

"This is gonna hurt." Lily sighed then took a deep breath.

"I will help you." Irene grabbed Lily's hand.

Captain Cory's Icicle had probably cleared or was close to clearing NP airspace at this point. Irene and Lily still had half the scaffold to climb.

"So much for the chase," Lily laughed again. The meds must have kicked in.

"We can catch up with your piloting skills no problem..." Irene stopped. She realized that Lily had just taken some major painkillers.

"Yes, I can do it." Lily's head bobbed a bit from exhaustion.

"How about you walk me through the launch? Later you can take over." Irene shook her head.

Lily shook her head. "No, no. I'm fine. I can do it."

They finally made it to the top of the scaffold and the Icicle ramp door. Irene tapped her palm on the pad next to the door then stepped back. Lily waited a few paces back and watched the ramp door drop to the scaffold.

"Let's do this." Lily and Irene entered the Icicle, turned right, and headed to the cockpit. The view port was raised to give a clear field of vision no matter what position the Icicle was in. It could hang vertically and fly horizontally so a versatile viewport was needed as well as the sophisticated swivel chairs that shift with the Icicle's dynamic position system as well.

Lily strapped herself in. Irene still watched her in

case, the painkillers proved too much for her. Irene sat in the co-pilot chair.

"Okay let's boot her up! She should have plenty of power. We didn't even get to fly her last Christmas." Lily hit the ignition. The launch engines coughed then settled into a dull roar. The lights on the cockpit's console lit up. Lily grabbed for headset and tapped her mic for testing. Irene did the same.

"Let's hit it." Lily initiated the launch sequence. The countdown clock started from 10 to 0.

"Wait, Lily! You didn't detach the superstructure from the side of the Icicle!" Irene yelled hoping there was enough time to abort launch before the metal scaffolding killed their thrust and cause a horrible crash.

"Whoops. Hit that red button."

The timer was already at five headed to four seconds 'til launch.

"What red button?!" Irene panicked.

The countdown read three.

Irene still struggled to see the red button.

Two.

"I got it." Irene pushed the red button in the center of the console between her and Lily.

The countdown timer went back to 10.

"Sheesh. Why didn't you just hit it, Lily?" Irene was frustrated.

Lily detached the superstructure from the Icicle. The Icicle was clear for launch.

"Now we can launch. Are we officially clear for launch Irene?" Lily turned to look at Irene.

"Yes, now we are good to go. We better get going they already have a head start."

"We still have the element of surprise."

The Icicle launched from the Hangar. The beautiful lights of the North Pole lay beneath them. They had no time for to gaze at the beauty below them. Lily initiated the horizontal-swing. She engaged the thrusters. Their swivel chairs moved with the Icicle. Their pursuit of Captain Cory began.

THIRTY-THREE
YELLOW PAGES

The snow began to fall once again. Jane was glad to have rest after using the Power Frenetic. She didn't know how much more she could push herself. A fairy needs her rest. There is no just no option. Fairy Freeze is an affliction that has struck many fairies throughout time. Wings will just give out at any moment, some during mid-flight at high altitudes. The fairies did not survive the fall. Jane pushed that possibility to the back of her mind. Her fellow Fae needed her. She would make it.

Jane rested on the Press Club rooftop waiting for Kath. She figured the falling was snow was indicative of her sister's return. She was happy to see her.

"I think I have something to go on." Kath landed next to her, excited.

"Good. Good. I tried calling Lily. My Admiral

answered, and said they are sending a Tailor Team to help us, but something about it just doesn't feel right. Anyway, what have you got?" Jane leaned over to look at Kath's phone.

"I was able to figure out the surveillance system pretty quickly. It seemed more advanced than the one you described or maybe you are just dumb." Kath laughed.

"Funny. Really funny. Lily said the White House would probably have a better system. Now what do you have? We don't have time to mess around. Come on."

"Whoa. Easy sister. A human is involved. Here take a look at this. I am pretty sure he lets out a phantom Fae right next to the tree." Kath showed Jane the photo.

"Oh great. A human! This is not good. How would a human even know about Fae? I thought our efforts with J.M Barrie to fictionalize us worked!" Jane stood up and paced the gravel rooftop.

"Relax. So far it seems we can contain the situation. There was only one human I saw. Before he pulled out the vial he carried the Fae in he pulled out an ID." Kath zoomed in on it.

"There is no way we can make out his name with this pixelated image." Jane scoured.

"This seems to be a work ID. There are three larger

letters above the blurry pic. Help me make the letters out and we can search." Kath reveled in her newfound sleuthing.

"Okay at least it's something. Looks like an 'O' or a 'Q' maybe? The second letter is a 'T' and the third..." Jane looked befuddled.

"It looks like an 'M' to me."

"So, it's either 'OTM' or 'QTM'. Humans still don't have public digital records yet. We are going to have to check the Yellow pages, right? That is where humans list their information?" Jane asked.

"Yes, there is a phone booth down on the corner there. Let's check for a listing, you never know." Kath jumped off the roof, spread her wings and descended toward the empty phone booth. There was steady traffic and a few pedestrians. The Solstice Fae didn't seem to care.

Jane shook her head and followed. Solstice Fae were more comfortable being around humans than North Pole Fairies. Perhaps too comfortable.

The phone booth door was open. Kath was underneath the pay phone in the cubby that held the giant book with yellow pages.

Jane entered. "Will you be just a little more careful, Kath. We don't want to attract more unwanted attention from humans."

Kath ignored her comments and started pushing the book out of the cubby.

"Come help me with this. The both of us can push this out easy."

Jane looked out of the phone booth at the sidewalk. It was clear. She then flew to the back of the cubby. There was a small space between the back of the phone cabinet and the book itself. The tiny fairies pushed the giant book with all their might. It barely budged.

"We just need to clear a bit more space then we can use our wings to push as well." Kath's back was to the spine of the book and she used her legs to push.

Jane reluctantly agreed, hoping her legs could help more than her wings. The book moved an inch.

They heard footsteps and a loud metallic clink followed by audible pounding. Someone was dialing.

"Stop!" Jane mouthed the command silently.

Kath didn't stop. She now flitted her wings. The book moved with greater speed and was about halfway out of the cubby.

The human's voice bellowed, "Yeah, hello, I will be there tonight at about 8, right? Outside of the Ford's Theat—" The voice stopped.

"What the? I gotta go! See ya later. There has to be a rat in this phone booth!" The banging sound was the human dropping the phone and running away.

Kath pushed the rest of the book out onto the ground of the phone booth.

She stood at the end of the shelf. "See humans are more scared than anything. We are fine."

"That was reckless and stupid, Kath. You would think being the older, wiser sister you would not make dumb moves like that." Jane stomped towards her.

"Oh, here we go. Same old argument. Do everything your way, which by the way, is Mom and Dad's way, Jane. I have more experience around humans and I know what I can and cannot get away with. This is why I left. I couldn't stand being around your perfection Jane," Kath said.

"Good. I was glad you left anyway. Made my life easier not having to feel guilty for always being better than you at everything." Jane was mad. Her words lacked truth but packed pain.

Kath's eyes watered but she wouldn't give her sister the satisfaction.

"Good luck working alone from here on out. I don't need your help." Kath flew down to the yellow book and with a rage opened it.

"Kath. I am sorry. I didn't mean it." Jane flew down next to her as Kath opened the heavy book all by herself to the letter 'Q'.

Kath examined the business and offices that started with the rarely used letter. There weren't many. The acronym 'QTM' was a research and development firm in the Smithsonian Institution.

Kath didn't say a word to Jane and upon finding the address flew out of the phone booth away from her sister.

Jane thought she should pursue but didn't. She knew where she was headed.

THIRTY-FOUR
PATCHED POWERLESS

Lily and Irene did a robust radar ping and they pinpointed the location of Cory's Icicle. They were in pursuit but stayed back a few miles to avoid confrontation. Cory would never suspect he was being followed. They headed south by southwest to D.C..

"How are you feeling Lily?" Irene asked keeping her eyes to the viewport.

"I am better but now aching more. Sorry about earlier, the pain meds were a bit stronger than I had anticipated," Lily said.

"Yes, the Hospital Branch doesn't mess around with injuries like that. I had a burn from a bubble light overheating and they hooked me up with some great meds. Any luck patching into Jane's com?"

"I am trying to hack my own encryption. I am too good. And well, I had the password saved on my GlimmerHack which is missing. It's taking forever even with the Icicle's antenna power. I don't think at this point I will be able to send any signals, but we may be able to hear her com." Lily punched a few more numbers and letters into the communication console. Her eyes widened.

Voices sounded into Lily's headset. She pushed a few buttons and ran the audio to the cockpit speakers, so Irene could hear.

"Cory, we have a solid lead on where the missing Fae might be stored. An R and D firm called QTM in the Smithsonian. I will need you to stand by and keep a flight pattern around the institution, in case, I need your help for extraction. Hopefully I'll have fairies to bring aboard," Jane said.

"Roger that, Jane. Glad we can be of assistance," Cory said.

"If you don't mind me asking, who is with you?" Lily and Irene looked at each other in recognition of Jane's careful tone. She suspected something was amiss.

"Will is here. And Julia. Pixie suggested I don't bring any outside help unless absolutely necessary."

"I am sure he did. He is always careful about covering his own ass. How long will it take you to get here?"

"We should be there in about an hour. We are

making great time in our Icicle. Over." Cory's tone was too friendly or at least it seemed so since Lily knew his true persona. In the academy he was much more relaxed in his tone, always nice but he didn't try so hard like he was now.

"Contact me when you are close, and I will give you the situation report. Out." Jane ended the com call.

Lily attempted to hail her, "Jane! Jane! Over?" She put her head in her hands.

"So, I take it we can only listen in and not break in, huh?" Irene asked.

"Yes. Ugh. The question is why is Cory doing this in the first place? And are all three Tailor captains aware of his scheme or is he setting them up too? Regardless, we can assume that Jane is headed straight into a trap."

"You think Cory is responsible for the missing Fae and he is trying to cover it all up?" Can we get to the Smithsonian faster than they can without alerting them?" Irene leaned forward and checked the power supply display of Icicle.

"Yes, he is responsible. Trying to have me killed by making it look like an accident then sending a lackey to the hospital to finish the job. Again, to what end? Why kidnap fairies? And are humans involved? If they are headed to the Smithsonian we can assume that humans must be involved? There are no Hollows at the Smithsonian. Can you use the onboard computer and find what you can on QTM, Irene?"

"I am on it."

"I am going to try to figure out a way to increase our speed and maintain our stealth. Now we are in a race."

THIRTY-FIVE
SMITHSONIAN

Jane flew over the National Mall. Daylight was burning to an end. The sun was setting behind the Washington Monument and the Lincoln memorial. She headed south to the administration building of the Smithsonian. It was a relatively non-descript gray building with multiple levels. It was a typical office building, but it served as a hub to a vast network of 17 world-class museums and exhibits, and even underground levels and tunnels filled with artifacts from around the world.

Jane flew into the lobby above the door security and looked for an office index. On a wall near the elevator banks, she read the sign. The only office with a 'Q' was located on sub-level 3.

The elevator emptied a few humans into the lobby as the end of the workday had arrived. Jane quickly flew in over their heads. The elevator closed. She was alone and flew to the floor list and punched the S3 button.

Jane took a cue from her sister and started to be less careful around the humans. They seemed too busy, preoccupied to notice a tiny fairy flying around. Perhaps by nature humans were too self-absorbed. Still, Jane wanted to maintain a certain degree of stealth especially since humans in this building might know of fairies.

The elevator opened to a brightly lit and banal hallway, with white walls and white and gray speckled flooring. Jane hoped to run into her sister. She felt a certain level of guilt and frustration. She had tried to apologize to Kath, but Kath had ignored her-- maybe, justifiably so. Still, Jane thought they worked better together. A common enemy and shared goals could help strengthen their relationship.

Jane hugged the ceiling and headed toward the suite number of QTM. She flew down a hallway that seemed to go on forever. Her heart began to beat a little faster at the prospect of the danger that lay ahead. Hopefully, her wings still had enough left in them. She had to be close.

At the end of the hall was an office door with, 'QTM' on the name plate.

Jane scanned the area around the door for a way in when the door opened.

The bearded man from White House feed emerged from the office. Must be quittin' time. He had a lab coat on. He stopped and searched his pockets for the keys to lock the door, but before he could Jane sprang into action and flew over his head and into the office. The door slammed behind her. The audible and ominous sound of the door's lock filled the room. Jane took a deep breath, in an attempt to calm her nerves. It looked like a typical office space. A receptionist's desk, a couple chairs that looked brand new and never used, and a hallway that led deeper into the office. Jane pushed forward down the hallway, into the darkness.

THIRTY-SIX
HOLLOW HOLLOW

Jane felt an impending sense of doom the further down the hallway she flew. The dread manifested itself quickly and in abundance. The lights turned on. Jane found herself in a vast laboratory. Hanging from the ceiling were transparent jars. In the jars, were the Fae. They had been imprisoned and were being used as lab experiments. Jane's stomach felt sick. She put a hand on her chest and the tears rolled down her face.

Suddenly, her view of the lab was obscured by the transition of six Phantom Fae appearing in a circle around her. There uniforms were steel grey. The masks secured to their faces just like in Solstice Hollow.

"I don't want to have to do this. I know this is not your fault. I know you are not really like this." Jane charged the phantom to her twelve o'clock. She employed the same tackle method as before. Jane aimed the phantom, writhing with pain over her shoulder onto a table with glass beakers and empty vials. Some of the vials rolled off and broke on the floor. Jane used so much force that she flew the phantom through a beaker.

Jane's Fae adrenaline coursed through her veins that she didn't notice the pain from her wings anymore. She dropped the phantom onto a shard of glass and turned to face the others.

They split up and engaged their invisibility DUST. Jane walked along the lab table with her fists charged ready to engage. She didn't want to overtax her wings and freeze them. She wanted to preserve as much energy in between bouts as she could.

Jane reached into her pocket and grabbed her own DUST. She spun in a circle and spread the DUST in a wide circle around her. Of course, it would not have the same effect on the phantom Fae as it did on humans but, there was enough in the air that the phantoms would reveal themselves if they entered her cloud. Her particles would show their outline.

One entered Jane's cloud of golden DUST on her left. Jane picked up a shard of broken glass and threw it at the phantom. The shard smacked against the phantom's face. It fell to the floor.

"Four more to go." Jane swirled around scanning the room for more phantoms. She spread more DUST.

The cloud refreshed. Jane kept moving in a circle. Sweat peppered her forehead. She threw off her leather aviator helmet and goggles and quickly ran her hands through her hair to keep it away from her face.

Another phantom pushed through the cloud but didn't move. Then another. Their outlines were surreal. Golden, dusted shapes like statues made from desert winds.

"Come on!" Jane commanded. She knew they were trying to surround her. The other two were behind her she could sense it. She had one last ditch strategy. The Power Frenetic. One more time. The other two phantoms attempted to grab her from behind. Jane knelt and pounded both her fists onto the table. Her wings flapped furiously with light, power, and pure magic.

"AHHHHH!" Jane flew straight up, knocking down all four of the golden-outlined phantoms. She then pulled back around and dove straight back down at the two who were getting back up.

She zeroed in and knocked one off the lab table with her landing. Jane then kicked the other phantom in the stomach so hard it reverted to its visible state and cowered in muffled agony under its mask.

The other two phantoms charged Jane. Jane hovered and didn't hesitate to tackle one. Jane carried the phantom straight across the table in a darting shot.

Once Jane cleared the table she dropped the phantom who was so dazed from the momentum of the tackle, it crashed to the floor.

Jane hovered a few inches off the ground and looked for the last phantom. Her glow was still strong. Her wings were still powerfully flapping.

"One left. Come on!" Jane's rage and adrenaline got the best of her. The last phantom Fae dropped the jar over her. Jane's light immediately went out. She was trapped. The bottom of the mason jar proved too strong of a glass ceiling for her to break through.

THIRTY-SEVEN
SISTER STEALTH

Jane couldn't believe her stupidity. She sat on the lab floor trapped in a mason jar. The same type of prison that hung from the ceiling and trapped her fellow Fae. Worse yet, Jane knew she had pushed her wings too far. She tried to flap them. The affliction she thought would never overcome her did. Her wings had frozen. She would not be able to fly without rest and medical attention from the doctors at the NP Hollow. She felt the immense weight of failure on her back, in her chest, almost everywhere. All she wanted to do was lay down and curl up in a ball.

Her captor, the phantom Fae, walked over to the jar and just waved her finger in the air as if to mock her.

"Very funny. You better pray that I don't find a way

out of this jar you savage." Jane's pride was impregnable to her enemies.

Jane looked around at sterile lab. There were many jars hanging from the ceiling. Coco had to be in one of them. Jane noticed syringes that she had knocked to the floor in her battle with the phantoms. Whatever was happening in this lab was turning good Fae into evil phantoms. The inhumanity of the human scientist sickened Jane.

She looked back at the phantom who stood guard. "Are you still here? I am obviously not going anywhere. Help us get out of here. Don't you know who you really are. He turned you into this. That man. QTM... this place is using us Fae for evil. Help us get out of here!"

The phantom just stared then folded its arms.

"That's all you got. Just fold your arms and stare." Jane rose to her feet.

The phantom Fae's head snapped back, and it started grasping at its own neck. It slowly dropped to the ground.

Jane was befuddled. Another phantom attacked its own?

Kath's raven-haired head appeared.

Jane held her hands over her mouth.

"Relax, idiot. I realized that their uniforms were the source of their invisibility DUST. So, I grabbed one off one of the fairies that you beat the heck out of. You do realize that these are our Fae you are fighting." Kath bent over to get a grip on the mason jar to free her sister but then decided to just knock it over.

"I am actually glad to see you for the first time in my life. Thank you. I am sorry. Really I am." Jane hugged her sister's invisible body.

"I guess I accept your apology. Come on we have to get all of these Fae out of here before more phantoms show themselves or that creepy human comes back."

"There's a problem. I-I can' t... fly. My wings are frozen. I have a solution though. Captain Cory's Icicle can fit all of us and fly us right out of here."

"That will have to work. Tell him to meet us at the Smithsonian Air and Space Museum. It's a short walk from here. That is how I sneaked in, well if you call using breach charges sneaking in." Kath was now completely visible.

"Wait, you snuck in? I just came in through the front door and the elevator and everything like I thought you would," Jane said.

"I mean I am bold around humans but not that bold."

"You said I needed to not be so afraid of humans!"

"No, I said, I know what I can and can't get away with around humans. I didn't say I fly among them and use their entrances, elevators, and exits Jane. You are lucky you made it this far." Kath looked around at the ceiling, counting with her hands.

"Ugh. Whatever. You are so frustrating."

"I count eight jars and eight Fae. I will get them down. You call in your Tailor rescue team. These Fae don't look fit to fly. They look emaciated."

THIRTY-EIGHT

SAFETY NOT GUARANTEED

Irene used her Lighting Tailor skills to great effect they used the Icicle's lights to emulate a human passenger airplane's lights. Irene and Lily then emptied their Icicle of any unnecessary cargo to increase speed and fuel efficiency and were keeping pace high above Cory's Icicle. If Cory were to look up Irene's light scheme would draw no suspicion. Icicles shared the skies with airliners all the time.

The speaker on Brendan's cockpit crackled with Jane's voice," Captain Cory. Over?"

Lily and Irene both listened in. The time to engage their element of surprise neared.

"This is Cory, Over. Jane, good to hear from you."

"We need to be picked up in the Smithsonian Air and Space Museum. The National Mall entrance. The

Milestones of Flight section. We will have at least eight additional passengers. You have room? Over."

"Yes, we do. We will be there shortly. Bout ten minutes. See you there. Out."

"Here we go. Now we know exactly where to go." Lily typed in the coordinates into the Icicle's flight deck.

"Think we can get there faster?" Irene pinged the radar once again.

"Looks like they are moving at max speed. We lightened our load though, so we should have the advantage. At the last minute we will drop altitude in front of them. As soon as we do that Cory will know the game is up. We will wait until he begins his descent toward the Air and Space Museum."

"What choice do we have?" Irene said.

"We don't. This is our shot. If we can move fast enough we can avoid the fight."

CAPTAIN CORY COULD FINALLY RELAX as Jane gave him her exact coordinates. He couldn't believe this containment plan took this long. He thought for sure QTM's eagle would have killed the investigation at Niagara. Things got messy, but the clean-up was about to happen. He looked over at his love, Julia; this was all for her. Well, most of it anyway.

"You can stop worrying now. Our Fairy Flyers have been found." Cory patted Julia's knee.

"I hope so." Julia looked out at the approaching lights of the National Mall, the Lincoln Memorial's temple-like structure, the oval open space of the World War II memorial, the massive obelisk of the Washington monument, and the magnificent rotunda of the Capitol building further in the distance.

"Will, start our descent. Air and Space is close," Cory said.

"THEY ARE DESCENDING LILY!" Irene said. She checked her seatbelt in the co-pilot chair.

"Here we go. Time to hit the boosters. Ready?" Lily gripped the flight stick and pitched the Icicle in a dive position. The tip of the Icicle faced downwards on an angle headed for the National Mall.

"Here we go." Irene unwrapped the booster bow on her chair.

BOOM!

Lily and Irene felt the immense pressure of the Icicle's boost engines. Lily managed to hang on and keep on the flight path.

"Are we over Cory, Irene?"

"We have definitely surpassed them and are currently beating them to the Air and Space

Museum. We will be in their viewport in a few seconds!"

THE UNKNOWN ICICLE dove ahead of theirs.

"What is that?" Cory asked loudly.

"It's another Icicle!" Captain Will yelled.

"I know that Will. I meant who is that?"

"We know who it is. It has to be Lily. We should have made sure she was taken care of." Julia prepped the boost function on their Icicle's flight deck.

THIRTY-NINE

VICTIM

Jane ran to Coco as soon as Kath flew her down from her prison jar.

Coco was weak. She was barely able to stand. Part of her hands and face looked discolored the same grey as the phantom Fae.

"Oh dear, Coco. What did they do to you?" Jane helped her stand.

"They were pumping chemicals into the jar every day for a few hours at a time. It turns you into one of their drones. I watched it happen to a few of the Solstice Fae." Coco coughed and leaned heavily on Jane.

"We figured as much. What else did you see?"

"Jane, we have all of them. Follow me." Kath interrupted.

Kath walked to the corner wall of the large lab.

There was the hole big enough for the Fae to fit through. Kath had used some breach explosives upon her entry to the lab. The party of ten moved together in a line with Kath in the lead. Jane and Coco brought up the rear.

"Before the scientist pumped the gas into our jars. He collected our blood several times and our DUST. Lord knows what they will do with it." Coco tried to walk a few feet on her own but couldn't.

"Coco, let me help you," Jane insisted.

She fell unconscious. She hit the ground hard.

"Coco!"

Jane picked her up, frozen wings and all. The other emaciated Fae looked back and wanted to help.

"You guys go ahead. I got her." Jane walked with all of Coco's weight resting on her shoulder. The pain in her frozen wings and everywhere else worsened but Jane owed Coco her life. Never leave a fairy behind.

FORTY
OUTGUNNED NOT OUTMANEUVERED

"We are beating them! We can do this!" Irene checked the radar.

"We are close to Air and Space! They are probably real pissed off! Haha." Lily laughed. The Smithsonian Castle's spires were right beneath them.

Irene couldn't believe her eyes. The enemy Icicle just blipped closer to theirs and fast on the radar screen.

"Uh Lil' they just caught up and are right behind us!"

"They must have used their booster bow. Hit 'em with your lights!" Lily kept the dive smooth. She could see the tall spire, the glass center, and the concrete wings of the Air and Space Museum.

Irene opened the aft engines up and burned the

emergency white phosphorus flares in an attempt to blind them.

The radar blip now moved back some, "That seemed to slow 'em down a bit!"

"Good because we are about to reach the entrance!"

"WILL, I need you to keep this Icicle steady!" Cory yelled. Will was Cory's best friend and would follow him anywhere, even into mortal danger.

"They burned their flares in my face!" Will was piloting the Icicle.

"Julia take control. Will take this!" Cory handed Will a weapon.

Will still rubbed his eyes of the blindness Irene's flares thrust upon him.

"Now remember the shooting range with Haynes. Point. Shoot. Squeeze don't pull," Cory loaded his weapon then hit the Icicle ramp. He secured a grappling hook, so he could safely lean out of the Icicle and shoot.

Will followed.

"Julia! Get us close enough so we can hit their aft engines!"

"Roger that!" Julia hit the boost a bit more to close

the gap. She noticed the Air and Space was only a few hundred feet down below.

LILY KEPT her dive straight and true. "We are almost there!"

A pelt.

Another pelt. An impact. Something hit the Icicle and continued to hit it.

Irene looked around. "What is hitting us?"

"It's coming from behind. I am getting major resistance all of a sudden on the stick!" Lily informed.

Irene opened the side ramp door. She leaned out to see when she noticed the flashes from their pursuant Icicle. Irene quickly hit the button to close the ramp door and dove away from the door.

"Lily they are using human guns! Somehow they have tiny human guns!"

"They got us. Get back to your seat and strap in. Get ready for a crash landing! They knocked out one of our engines!"

FORTY-ONE
A SIGHT FOR SORE EYES

Jane carried Coco. Kath led the rest of the former prisoners to a freight elevator underneath the Air and Space Museum.

"Everybody aboard?!" Kath said while flying up to push the main floor button.

Jane gave a thumbs up as the rest of the Fae made it aboard the corrugated metal floor of the elevator. Jane carefully laid Coco down. Jane still held her head.

Kath pushed the button. The elevator ascended.

"She will be just fine, Jane. We are almost there. The Icicle will be waiting for us right outside." Kath flew down from the buttons and comforted her sister.

"I hope so. The Icicle should have some first aid onboard. At least enough to get these Fae some fluids." Jane looked at her fellow fairies. They were so tired, hungry, and yet they still managed to look out for each other.

"Thank you, Jane."

"Thank you, Kath."

A few more gestures of gratitude came out of their mouths.

Kath and Jane looked at each other.

"We are almost out of here to safety. An Icicle will pick us up when we reach the ground floor," Kath said.

A voice crackled through Jane's com.

"We are right outside Jane. We are ready for you. Over. All set there?" Cory asked.

"Yes, yes. Please prep the medical kits and all the water you have aboard. We will need all of it. Over."

"Yes, we are ready. Out."

Jane noted how abrupt Cory was. She didn't even know if she liked this Tailor or not. She wished Lily was the one picking them up.

The elevator doors opened.

Jane picked Coco back up onto her shoulders. Kath led them down a long hallway and into the Milestones of Flight Hall: The Spirit of St. Louis, the plane that Lindbergh flew across the Atlantic. The Bell X-1 which broke the sound barrier. The X-15, the jet that reached the edge of space, were on display in the grand exhibition room. The study of human aviation history was a requirement in the Fae academy and one of

Jane's favorite subjects. Humanity could be impressive at times.

Kath led them to the handicapped entrance and clicked the proper button leading them out on the front entrance. The museum had been closed for two hours already. The entrance steps were clear of humans.

The Icicle hovered. The ramp door was open. Cory stood in the door way.

"Come on in!"

FORTY-TWO
ENTRAPMENT

Kath and Cory helped the last Fae that was capable of walking on their own power into the Icicle.

Jane and Coco came next. Jane didn't feel right. It wasn't like Lily to not be thorough and just hand over the reins to Pixie and these other Tailors. She stopped at the bottom of the ramp with Coco on her shoulder.

"Here let me grab her." Cory walked down the ramp to help.

"No, no I got her." Jane looked at Kath.

Kath could sense her sister's reluctance to board.

"Are you sure? It is really no problem at all." Cory insisted.

"No, no, I brought her this far. I can take care of her myself." Jane took one step onto the ramp.

"Jane! No!" A familiar voice sounded in the distance.

"Jane! For the love of God. Do not get on that Icicle!" The voice was closer.

It was Lily's voice. Kath and Jane looked at each other. Jane stepped back from the ramp and put Coco down.

"Will!" Cory yelled.

Will stepped out of the Icicle with a gun aimed at Kath, Jane, and Coco.

Lily was close but still on the other side of the entrance. She limped.

"All we really need is the Fae we have on board. You understand? Your friend Coco was a bonus after you survived the eagle attack. Just let us fly away and all will be well."

"Jane! He tried to kill me. He's trying to cover up his connection to the abductions. I don't know why but they filed the reports to save face. He didn't think Pixie would actually do anything about it."

"Julia, get the Icicle ready to go. Close the ramp. I will catch up with you later," Cory said.

The aft engines of the horizontal Icicle sparked on. Will stopped aiming the gun at the Fae as the ramp door began to close. Cory jumped off and produced a handgun he had had hiding on his back.

"Let me explain. Julia's father is sick. The only way to heal her father is with Fairy blood and magic. This human scientist I heard about here in D.C. specializes in genetic engineering, among other things. We made a deal. I get him some Fae in exchange for the cure for Julia's father. He also offered a lot of money for each additional Fae we could capture. Apparently, your kind have powerful properties useful in many circles. Then we blend in with humanity and live a charmed life."

Lily hobbled closer.

"Now, I think he is telling the truth. Julia's father is sick!"

Cory shot a round at Lily. He missed.

"You son of a bitch!" Jane yelled. Cory quickly turned the gun back on Jane, Kath, and Coco.

"Don't move. Like I said. We are happy with the Fae we have on board. So, you four can just be on your merry way. No one gets hurt."

The Icicle took off carrying the sickly Fae back into QTM's hands.

"Kath. Do it." Jane shot her sister a look.

Kath spun quickly away and shot a beam of cold air at Cory's gun. Cory tried to squeeze the trigger. Kath used her Solstice power to freeze the gun.

"Get him!" Jane yelled.

"Buzz off! I bet your wondering how I got that human gun. Let me show you. QTM's tech has been amazing and has freed me from being a tree elf." Cory tapped his neck. He closed his eyes and began to grow taller and bigger before their eyes. Jane, Kath, and Lily were in awe but terrified at the same time. Cory was growing into the size of an adult human.

FORTY-THREE
GIANT PROBLEM

"Run Jane! I will get Coco to Lily's Icicle!" Kath picked Coco up from the ground. She ignored the massive tree elf's shoe right next to them.

"Jane! Let's go! Irene is rewiring Brendan's Icicle to put power back in our aft engines!" Lily hobbled back towards the landscaping she emerged from. Jane followed suit.

Cory's rapid growth had stopped. He could smash Jane and Lily with just a couple steps and he knew what to look for.

Jane ran as fast as she could.

"I really didn't want to have to do this. You left me no choice but to squash you, Jane. You have been really bugging me anyway." Cory's human size gave him tremendous power over the tiny Fae.

"Of all the days to freeze your wings Jane! You—

you pick today!" Jane yelled at herself while running as quickly as she could.

From a bush on the right side of the Air and Space Museum's entrance. Jane could see the aft engines of the Icicle light up.

Cory's first step missed. Jane ran diagonally when she saw him lift his foot.

The second stomp clipped her wing. She fell to the ground.

"Uh oh. I got you now!" Cory grimaced as he lifted his right foot for the final kill.

Jane looked up to see a glowing blue streak headed right for his foot. It was Kath.

Her sister's momentum knocked his foot back. He stumbled and almost tripped into the bush where the Icicle was.

"I can take care of King Jackass here. Get our Fae back!" Kath yelled down to Jane.

Jane picked herself up and ran to the ramp door of the Lily and Irene's commandeered Icicle.

"Good to see you Fairy Flyer!" Irene greeted her as she walked in.

Lily was back in the pilot seat.

Irene stood watch over the radar.

"Really wonderful to see you too Irene. Where is Julia's Icicle?"

"We have it on the radar it is moving towards the Capitol Building," Irene answered.

"We are back at full engine power. Good job Irene. In pursuit now. Jane get in one of those swivel seats and strap in," Lily said.

FORTY-FOUR
CAPITOL CRIMES

Jane hoped Kath was okay. She felt as if she would be. She could fly circles around Cory. She was more concerned about her original mission: the missing Fae. She looked over at Coco, who was still unconscious in the swivel seat next to her.

"Are we gaining on them?" Jane asked.

"Yes, they are carrying much more weight and when I rewired I took some extra juice from the onboard lights to give us more engine power," Irene answered.

Lily could see the Icicle in her view. It headed straight to the beautifully lit dome of the US Capitol Building.

"How do we get it down safely without killing the Fae on board?" Jane's mind moved 800 miles a minute.

"We are gonna use the extra GlimmerLifts on

board to grapple the Icicle on the side where there is no ramp door. We can pull it down. Or you can just fly over and wreak havoc on it?" Irene said.

"If only I could fly. I overused my wings. They are frozen."

"GlimmerLifts it is then. Are you going to be okay?" Irene shook her head.

"Yes, it happens from time to time." Jane ran her fingers through her hair again to keep it away from her face. She had ditched her helmet a while back now. She was tired. Her headache had returned.

"We are on approach. Irene, better get that door open and prep the grappling hooks. Julia is gaining altitude. It looks like she is planning to go right over the Statue of Freedom." Lily kept a steady pace and move alongside Julia's Icicle.

The ramp door opened. Irene prepped six GlimmerLifts or grappling hooks the Tailors use to traverse the Christmas trees they tend to.

"Jane, I will shoot the ones on the right side of the door. You get the ones on the left. After the hook connects, wrap the shooting mechanism around the hinges of the ramp door. Got it?" Irene's curly hair blew in the wind.

"I got it!" Jane settled into her position, grabbed a hook and readied her first shot. Irene the same.

"Hit it!" Irene yelled.

They both shot the hooks into the side of Julia's Icicle and wrapped the other end of the line on the hinge.

In unison they grabbed another. The hooks sank into the side of the Icicle.

"One more set should do it!" Irene grabbed for the last GlimmerLift when the Icicle shifted. Irene fell out onto the ramp. Jane grabbed the side of the doorway and reached for Irene. She held her wrist.

"Lily! Get us level now or Irene will die!" Jane yelled.

"I am trying! Don't let go of her." Lily reached for the button to ignite the side hover engines to right the ship.

Julia's Icicle attempted to pull away again. Irene was almost hanging only from Jane's grip and not the ramp.

Jane held the support bar next to the ramp door with her left hand and Irene with her right.

"Lily! Hurry!"

"I got it." Lily pushed a button and the hover engines burned for a few seconds. The ship was back to level. Jane felt comfortable enough to use both hands to pull Irene back in.

"Thank you, Jane!"

"No problem. I think four grapples is enough to bring Julia down," Jane said.

"I think so too." Irene and Jane ran back to their respective seats and strapped in.

"It's all you Lily!" Irene said.

CORY SWATTED AND SWATTED. He couldn't catch Kath. His bigger body caused his reflexes to slow. His new, human size also played hell with his mind-body coordination.

Kath hit pressure points all over his body again and again. His temples. His neck. His legs and occasionally his face for good measure.

She flew down to hit him in the balls. She did.

He cowered over. She then flew out and went for his face again. He caught her. She was inside of his fist.

"I got you! You little insect."

LILY ATTEMPTED a general hailing of Julia in her Icicle--pilot to pilot via the communication antenna.

"Julia, we have you grappled. Please land your Icicle immediately. I repeat we have you grappled with four GlimmerLifts off your starboard. Please desist now."

"You will kill us all. Detach your GlimmerLifts now," Julia answered.

Lily didn't want to get into a wrestling match in mid-air.

"Julia land with us now and we will see to it you get a more lenient sentencing in your court martial."

Julia punched the accelerator and headed straight to the top of the Statue of Freedom, the nineteen-foot statue perched high atop the Capitol Building.

"Hold on! She is not cooperating. I am going to stay with her 'til we get closer to the Statue of Freedom."

KATH LAY PRONE in the vice of Cory's fist. She waited until he opened his hand to give the order.

She glowed bright blue. Cory's palm pinged with freezing temps. The rest of Kath's Solstice Fae surrounded and swarmed him.

"No!" He yelled flailing his arms.

A blue glowing swarm attacked Cory. They brought their coldest temps. Some held and threw ice spears. Others formed ice blocks around his ankles. He fell to the ground. His head smacked against the concrete.

"Nice work, Fae. I think we got him."

As he fell unconscious he shrank back to his minuscule tree elf form.

"Three of you lock him up in the Hollow for now. The rest of you come with me."

FORTY-FIVE

FREEDOM REIGNS

Lily knew exactly what Julia was hoping to do. She was going to try to use the bronze feathers atop the Statue of Freedom to sever the lines from the GlimmerLifts.

Jane detached her seatbelt and walked next to Lily.

"Lily, tell me when you are gonna hit the brakes. Will has a gun in there. We can assume is pointed right at our Fae. If we can use the moment you hit the reverse thrusters, maybe, they can find the energy to wrestle the gun away from him and take the ship back. Give me your headset."

"Sounds like a good a plan as any. Make sure to keep it short. She will cut you off as soon as she can" Lily handed Jane the headset.

They neared the top of the Statue of Freedom.

"Hitting reverse thrusters now. All yours, Jane." Jane almost fell, due to the shift in momentum.

"Fellow Fae! Now is your chance. Take back the Icicle! Now!" Jane hoped it went through.

"She is still trying push us forward. If I keep resisting, we might destroy both of our Icicles. Or the lines won't hold, and she will get away and we start from square one," Lily said.

"Hang on just a bit longer. If their Icicle pulls back then we know they might have gotten my message," Jane said.

The first line snapped. Julia's Icicle surged more to Lady Freedom's star-laden helmet.

"Hang on just a little bit longer Lil'!"

The second line snapped. The third line bent the hinge on the ramp door.

The third line detached.

"Jane, we have to give up or we lose any..." Lily's Icicle started pulling away from the Statue of Freedom with Julia's Icicle in tow.

"Wait she gave up! They did it. They must have taken the ship back!"

Jane and Irene screamed with delight, "WOO HOO!"

"Try hailing them again!" Lily lowered the Icicles away from the top of the Capitol Building.

"Thank you for complying. Please fly with us

down to Capitol lawn. With whom am I speaking too?" Jane asked.

"This is Veronica of the Fairy Fleet. We have taken back the Icicle. I repeat we will comply. We have taken back the Icicle."

"Great to hear Fairy Flyers! Wonderful. Just wonderful." Jane burst into happy tears. Irene embraced her. She looked over at Coco. She was stirring.

"What is with all the yelling?" Coco asked as she rubbed her head.

"We won Coco. Everyone is safe." Jane sat next to her.

"Oh, looks like we have a fairy escort." Lily pointed to the viewport.

A beautiful collection of Solstice Fae with their blue glow, helped guide the Icicles down to the Capitol lawn.

Jane and Irene ran out onto the ramp to check out the missing Fae's Icicle.

Kath joined, "How did you get them to stand down?"

"We didn't." Jane pointed to the ramp door, "They did."

The missing Fae were now found and doing their duty.

Veronica stood at the entrance of the ramp with

Will's rifle in her hand. She wobbled a bit but was able to keep her balance.

Kath directed two of the Solstice Fae to get Julia and Will.

"How did you do it, Veronica?" Jane asked

"On your cue we were already using whatever energy we had left to tackle Will. The pull of your Icicle caused him to drop the gun. It slid to me and I picked it up. Julia then really had no choice after that." Veronica looked at the gun and threw it out onto the grass.

"Great work, Fairy Flyer. Great work."

Kath, Jane, and Irene helped the weakened Fae over to Lily's Icicle. Their bodies were somewhat frail, but their spirits were strong. Four Solstice Fae and three fairies from the Fleet joined Coco.

"I think that's everybody. Everyone important anyway," Kath said.

Will was escorted about by a Solstice Fairy. He looked dazed and confused like he didn't know what hit him.

Julia followed. She was crying hysterically. Her plan to find a way to cure her father's condition was misguided. She kept muttering, "I just wanted to help him. I just wanted to help him."

Jane rolled her eyes.

"She really doesn't have to make it out of this alive you know?" Kath joked.

Jane laughed.

FORTY-SIX
REPERCUSSION AND REMEMBRANCE

The sisters Fae walked toward the Icicles landed near Kath's Solstice Hollow on Theodore Roosevelt Island. The sun shined, and a new winter's day was upon them.

"If my Hollow wasn't so messed up and compromised I would keep them here. I want to keep them here after what they did to my Fae," Kath said, bitter from her Fae being turned evil.

"I understand but the Icicle brig will keep them secure and we will put them through the court martial process. They are technically, Tailors," Jane said.

"What do we do about QTM and the creepy bearded guy?"

"Maybe after I do my debrief the Fleet can send its resources to help or you can do whatever you like." Jane smiled.

"You mean you aren't going to give me any orders? Wow. Maybe you aren't such an idiot after all," Kath laughed.

"I have no power or jurisdiction over you. Clearly. No, but seriously, thank you so much for all your help."

"I suppose we did a thing together. A good thing. We work well together."

"Are we going to take it that far, ya think?" Jane stopped walking.

"I don't know what the heck I was thinking. You are right. We are the worst."

Jane laughed.

Kath followed suit.

"Hey, you know there is always a place for you in the Fleet."

"Right back at you little sister. And you know what it looks like you have plenty of amazing sisters. Lily, Irene, Coco, what do you need me for?"

Jane walked up the ramp of the Icicle.

"Hey Kath, we don't say this enough as actual blood siblings... I love you."

"Love you too, now get out of here already."
***

For more adventures with Jane, Lily, and Irene check out the Tannenbaum Tailors saga at mistermichaels.com.

ABOUT THE AUTHOR

JB Michaels is an award-winning and USA Today Bestselling Author of two series: Bud Hutchins Thrillers and the Tannenbaum Tailors.

JB has spent his life in the study of story from riveting novels to the slam-bang action-packed world of comics to the examination of film history. JB has spent a lifetime learning and examining the elements that make a story incredible. This steadfast dedication has led him to writing stories of his own.

JB is married and with a son, he has a great love of family.

For more stories filled with action, thrills, and heart (oh and a FREE book or two) please visit MisterMichaels.com

Made in the USA
Monee, IL
29 August 2020

40380019R00111